MW01004791

SWORD OF OAK

DRAGONS RISING BOOK FOUR

ALISHA KLAPHEKE

Copyright © 2020 by Alisha Klapheke

All rights reserved.

No part of this book may be reproduced in any form or by any electronic
or mechanical means, including information storage and retrieval
systems, without written permission from the author, except for the use
of brief quotations in a book review.

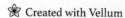 Created with Vellum

For Amelia and Aidan whose creativity and caring amaze me

JADE CAVES

Silver River

LAPIS CAVES

RED MEADOW

Bihotzetik
(SUNKEN CITY)

FIRE MARSHES

DRAGON'S BACK

THE GREAT SEA

FOREST OF ILLUMAURAH

Lost Valley

SUGARRABOTA ISLE

CAST OF CHARACTERS

Humans

Vahly—twenty-three years of age, the only survivor of her kynd

Lapis Dragons

Amona—Matriarch of the Lapis Clan

Maur—male noble warrior, daughter in line to be next Matriarch

Helena—female healer

Ruda—female youngling

Linexa—female who cares for younglings

Xabier—newly matured male warrior

Elixane—deceased Matriarch with legendary hoard

Lys—female librarian

Draes—male librarian

Eneko—male noble

Rip—male palace guard

Ty—male palace guard

Jade Dragons

Eux—Matriarch of the Jade Clan

Zarux—male noble warrior

Call Breaker Dragons

Nix—female smuggler, spy, owner of cider house

Dramour—male former warrior who is devoted to Nix

Ibai—male healer

Kemen—male healer and muscle

Aitor—male spy and thief for Nix, scar, black hair

Euskal—male former warrior

Miren—female former warrior

Baww—male who manages cider house

Elves

Arcturus—royal male alchemist

Vega—ancient female guard

Pegasi—young male guard

Leporis—male guard

Mattin—King of the Elves

Canopus—the King's right hand

Cassiopeia—royal female strategist

Regulus—elder and warrior

Rigel—male scout, silver-haired, member of Council

Haldus—male host and warrior, brown hair, short for an elf

Deneb—female devoted to the King

Gruis—male courtier

Ursae—female courtier

Sea Folk

Ryton—male consort to the Sea Queen, High General

Astraea—the Sea Queen

Grystark—male General

Venu—male General

Sansya—young female warrior

Echo—female scout

Calix—male scout

Selene—deceased female warrior, sister to Ryton

Lilia—female craftsfolk, wife to Grystark

Yenn—female warrior

Gracus—male scout

CHAPTER 1

One thousand, two hundred, fifty-five Lapis dead.

The number pierced Vahly's heart. What had it been like inside the Lapis cave palace when the Sea Queen's spelled salt water crashed through the doors?

Younglings reaching for their mothers. Spells blackening the dragons' scales. The kitchen staff trying to reach the back door when a wave punches them backward, burning their wings with the sea folk's magic. Warriors and their families gathered in the hall suddenly deluged by spelled seawater. The dragons lift into the air, but the waves charge higher and higher until there is no more room. The oculus is too narrow to fit more than one escaping dragon at a time. Screams. Gurgling. Lungs eroding. Eyes closing for the last time, fingers trailing away from a loved one's hand as the water rises and rises and rises.

"Vahly?" Arc lifted his black eyebrows. His elven crown shifted just out of sight, the golden threads of light and smoky tendrils at his forehead reaching upward.

Vahly shivered. "Oh, sorry. Yes, Aitor should come with us if he wants. Of course."

Arc's eyes softened and he tilted his head. "You already said that. We were asking about possible routes to Illumahrah, to the Sacred Oak."

"Right." She shook her head, but the images cut into her mind again and again. Clearing her throat, she joined Arc, and they started toward Nix, Aitor, and Amona.

The Jade clan's matriarch, Eux, descended from the sky in her human kynd form, bright green scales glittering in the sun and wings the color of the southern hills at dusk. The three Jades with her threw more bags of supplies at Arc's feet. A scorchpepper rolled from one satchel to land near Amona.

Also in her human form, Amona left the boulder she'd been sitting on to approach Eux. Her eyes narrowed at her former enemy, lips twisting like she was keeping some harsh words from escaping.

"Thank you, Matriarch Eux," Amona said instead. "Your generosity speaks highly of you and your clan."

Vahly and Nix traded a look. Never once had Amona spoken so kindly to Eux. Vahly prayed Eux would return the respect.

Smoke curled from Eux's delicately scaled nostrils as she strode over, arms crossed. Links made from jade stone framed her face and ran down her arms. Each ring held the tooth of a lost loved one, and while the sentiment was honorable, the sight of the memory links was horrifying. A ruby sparkled from the hilt of Eux's sword. Beside her, Amona looked plain.

Vahly's dragon mother had lost everything material during the battle. Her sword. Her beloved jewelry. And she'd lost most of her clan. Amona stood straight though, sharp eyes set on Eux.

Eux cocked her head and looked Amona up and down. "If you had fought harder earlier, perhaps we would be in a better position just now."

Amona's hands fisted as she stepped forward, her nose inches from Eux's face.

Vahly took a step. The air crackled, and the scent of dragonfire—citrus and charcoal—combined with the chill breeze.

"Do not," Amona hissed, "speak of fighting. That day, we fought like no other dragon. My Lapis survived because we put one another first. We would all be gone if we hadn't fought like true Lapis. The Jades would be long dead if they had been thus attacked."

Eux's wings spread and fire erupted from her lips. Amona lifted into the air, striking out and slicing Eux's cheek open with a talon. Blood splattered to the icy ground.

Vahly ran between them, the dizzying heat of dragonfire barely missing her. "Stop!"

Amona's battle-glazed eyes remained focused on

Eux. She roared and shot fire at the Jade matriarch, who dodged the blaze and leapt into the air. The two dragons locked in combat above Vahly.

They had sworn themselves to her. She had to stop this.

Arc, Nix, and Kyril were holding the Lapis back, a barrier of elf and dragon and gryphon between Amona's clan and Eux's.

Vahly knelt and put her palms on the earth. As she closed her eyes, the earth answered her touch with three powerful drumbeats of magic inside her chest. Flexing her hands, she stood and backed away.

The earth shot into the air.

A wall of stone shaped like a dragon broke Amona and Eux apart. The matriarchs sputtered fire and rolled, wings tucking. Eux and Amona landed on either side of Vahly's creation.

Amona blinked. "Daughter. Earth Queen. I ..."

Eux stormed away from the stone dragon, toward Vahly, shoulders heaving and wings shuddering. Kyril launched forward and rose up on hind legs, towering over Eux.

Eux's lip curled. "Peace, gryphon. I relent." The Jade matriarch's burning gaze found Vahly. "Apologies, Earth Queen." Her tone said she was less than remorseful. Eux glanced at Amona as the Lapis matriarch joined them. "We are one clan now, and you remind us of the fact." Eux dipped her head, then turned.

Amona bowed her head briefly. "Apologies, Earth Queen. I must remember my place. We are one."

Vahly reached a hand out to Amona, who didn't appear to be seriously injured though her clothing was singed and ripped down the side. Amona took her fingers and rubbed Vahly's wrist with a thumb. Amona's smile calmed Vahly's racing heart.

"It will take time, Daughter. Time for us to adjust. It would be good if I came with you to Illumahrah and left Eux to rule here."

"Agreed. I want you with me regardless."

With one more quick smile, Amona left, heading for Arc's remaining kynd—Haldus, Rigel and Ursae. They had been healing the Lapis rescued from the spits of land Vahly had raised during the battle. Young Ruda brought Amona what appeared to be a stack of fresh clothing.

Kyril shuffled over to Vahly and nudged her shoulder. She touched the smooth end of the gryphon's beak and exhaled, keeping an eye on the Jades who were gathering around Eux. Arc lifted his eyebrows at Vahly as if asking what he should do. She waved him over.

Vahly's boots crushed the icy grit of their vantage point of the northern mountains. Magic surged inside her, torn between going farther north into those snow-topped peaks and heading south toward Illumahrah to find the Sacred Oak.

Arc put a hand on her back, his touch warm. "What is it?" Formed of dark purple magic and dazzling golden light, his elven crown shimmered at his temples and across his forehead. The wind tugged at his ebony hair, and he narrowed his dark eyes against the cold.

"My magic is telling me to go north," she said.

"But what about the Sacred Oak and what Kyril saw?"

Vahly glanced at her familiar. The gryphon had curled up beside her, seemingly comfortable despite their position so high above the flooded remains of Sugurrabota.

Earlier, through telepathic communication, Kyril had shown her an image of the Sacred Oak at Illumahrah, the destroyed home of the elves. A field of yellow flowers had surrounded the tree where Vahly was meant to complete her journey to becoming a true Earth Queen, one capable of fighting the Sea Queen and thus balancing the world.

"I still have to visit the oak, but..." Magic pushed at her again, and she turned so that the highest of the snowy peaks filled her view. The mountains would have once made Vahly feel small. But now...

Tipped in blindingly white snow, the jagged rocks rose into the clouds. "First, there's something I must do."

CHAPTER 2

The mountains called to Vahly, her magic tugging at her.

Arc nodded. "The others will argue about heading in the opposite direction."

"I don't blame them." Vahly pulled her cloak more tightly around her body. One of the Jade clan dragons had brought the garment. "It won't be delightful for any of us." The mountain winds whistled. "I'm as eager as any of them to get going. The idea of going up there... It feels counterproductive, but for me, it also feels necessary."

She walked across the flat rock, and the entire group of survivors faced her, eyes expectant and wide.

A cold knife stabbed Vahly's gut. If she failed them, the ocean would rise to swallow the last of the land kynd. "I have to journey farther into the mountains before we leave for Illumahrah."

The Lapis-blue scales of Aitor's scarred face twisted. "All respect, Earth Queen, but what in the name of the Blackwater is worth us freezing our tails off in that empty land of ice?"

"I can't tell you that, unfortunately," Vahly said, "but my magic is urging me to go."

"We should move toward the oak and your final step in waking your earth magic, Queen Vahly. That," he said, eyeing the mountains, "will be a waste of time."

Nix smacked the back of Aitor's head. "If Queenie wants to shake her arse at the earth's last snow cat, we'll support her and make no mistake!"

Aitor scowled amid everyone's quiet chuckles, but he bowed his head. "Whatever you wish, Earth Queen."

Nix grinned at Aitor, then winked at Vahly.

Kyril lifted his eyes, his blue-gray feathers ruffling. A clicking sound came from his beak, and he stretched his front lion paws, digging claws into the stone and sending debris sifting into the air as he showed Vahly an image of them flying above a cliff lined in sparkling icicles.

Amona stepped forward, Ruda and Helena the healer flanking her. A deep emerald-green cloak similar to Vahly's fluttered around Amona's shoulders, and she wore a simple dress hemmed in the Jade symbol, the dragon skull's golden thread blinking in the sun. To see Amona in Jade clothing...

"Thus far," Amona said, "your magic has led you to success. Follow your instincts, Daughter, and we'll continue to follow you."

Vahly bowed her head.

Eux grunted but nodded. She hadn't changed out of her fire-blackened clothing. "Do you want the Jades with you, Earth Queen?"

Shaking her head, Vahly handed off her quiver and bow to Haldus, who gave her a sheepish smile. "I'll be fine with just my sword. So I believe it would be best to travel with a small group. Can your Jades instead continue looking for survivors and hunting to feed the rest?"

"Of course." Eux's orange eyes shifted to look at Amona.

The air tasted like smoke.

Amona dipped her chin. "Thank you, Matriarch Eux."

Nix handed a scorchpepper to young Ruda, who gobbled it down quickly. "Queenie," Nix said, "Those peaks aren't getting any less icy. I say we pack, eat a big meal, then move on."

"Agreed," Vahly said. "Arc, I mean, King Arcturus, Mistress Nix, Matriarch Amona, and Aitor, gather your supplies, if you will. And if you've decided you don't wish to risk the mountains, let me know. I won't force anyone."

Most of the dragons flew off to hunt the surrounding chilly climes.

Arc helped Vahly tuck dried goat meat, skins heavy with fresh water, and burlap sacks of raisins into two large satchels that they then slung over their shoulders. Over that, Arc slid the bow Haldus and Rigel had crafted for him from a stash of prepared wood the Jades had provided. A leather quiver of arrows pressed with the elven symbol of a sun and moon hung at his wide belt beside a short sword. Aitor had been unable to speak as he'd handed the weapons over that morning to her and to Arc. Vahly hadn't prodded him to find out whose swords they had been. She'd kissed the hilt and promised to do her best to honor the weapon's first wielder. She missed her own sword, lost to the sea, another precious memory drowned.

The hunters brought back five speckled rams, a brace of hares, and a good haul of eggs in varying colors. They set to butchering so portions could be divvied out to every dragon as well as the elves.

The Jades didn't bother roasting their meat even when in their human form. They sat on boulders and stumps, blood in their teeth. Vahly, shuddering at the sight, was plenty glad they were on her side now.

The Lapis and the Call Breakers gathered around fires and put their meat on spits the elves had fashioned. The meat cooked slowly to succulent perfection, seasoned with what appeared to be a local herb, bright green and with the scent of pepper.

Vahly's mouth watered as she sat down to a wide leaf covered in strips of steaming rabbit and a mess of fried eggs. Her stomach rumbled. She felt like she could eat as much as a dragon.

Once they'd finished up all there was at hand, Vahly took her turn at the makeshift privy—a trench dug at the base of the high-altitude spot they'd claimed as their base for operations. With all basic needs taken care of, the group readied to leave.

The sun reached its zenith, and Kyril launched into the sky, Arc and Vahly on his lion's back, his gray-blue eagle wings impossibly wide on either side of them. Nix, Amona, and Aitor flew in an arrow-shape beside them, blue wings like rain-heavy clouds on the horizon. They had bags of warm clothing and supplies clutched in their talons so they could transform into their human forms upon landing if they chose to do so.

Arc's kynd—Haldus, Ursae, and Rigel—waved a farewell from below. Ruda lifted a hand toward Kyril, her eyes shining. Vahly smiled down at the young Lapis. Ruda was Kyril's Sourceparent, and Vahly was glad that her familiar had another good soul to rely on if things went badly.

The wind went from stingingly chilly to bone-cracking cold as they soared above a high plateau of ice-slicked rock. In the distance, three craggy peaks speared steely clouds that swept in to cloak the sun. Magic pushed against Vahly's heart.

"There!" she called to Arc and pointed to the rest. "I have to visit those peaks."

Arc's hands tightened on her waist, and she leaned back, soaking in the heat and power of his presence. His sun-warmed sap-and-mint scent teased her nose, and her muscles relaxed.

"This is a place of legends," he said into her ear, the

wind trying to snatch his beautifully accented words away.

A gust swept up and Kyril veered, his warm body moving expertly to use the drafts and slide under the air currents.

"I'm scared to ask which legends," Vahly said.

"It is said the Blackwater takes a different form in the ice realms and affects wanderers in unique ways that other kynd rarely experience."

Frowning, Vahly gripped the furry ruff that ringed Kyril's neck, the feathers of his neck and head shifting in the wind. Rare experiences were over-praised. She needed power to end this war with Astraea before more good kynd fell. Even though magic urged her to travel into this white world, her spirit sagged as they flew closer to the three peaks. The sun, battling the clouds, showed over half the day gone already.

Exhaling, Vahly closed her eyes only to see an image Kyril sent to her. The image showed Vahly with a glowing chest like her heart was on fire. A flame extended from her and into the peaks.

Smiling, she leaned forward. "I hope that means you think this is the right move, Kyril. Because I'm not entirely sure."

Kyril lifted his head and gently bumped Vahly like he was trying to comfort her. Indeed, a surge of power flowed from her familiar's pelt into her palms.

Amona flew forward in a rush and jerked her dragon

head toward the east. The clouds had gone black over the peaks. Arc's hands gripped Vahly's waist in warning.

A storm was heading right for them.

CHAPTER 3

Vahly's stomach turned. "We need to figure out what's there, then leave before we're buried in snow."

"Quickly, Kyril," Arc called out.

Kyril flew faster, and the rest of the group followed suit, and soon they were landing on a slender outcropping on the first peak. Powdered snow covered the landing spot, heaping around Kyril's furred legs.

Vahly remained on Kyril's back while Arc dismounted. The area held nothing but sparse trees, stone, and snow. The narrow trail leading away from the outcropping showed that some forsaken beasts actually lived here and took this path from range to range. Her stomach turned. This was a fool's errand. She'd misread her magic's pull.

Beyond them, near Aitor and Amona, Nix's foot slipped off the path, and Vahly's stomach turned.

"Nix!" Vahly kicked her feet into Kyril's sides, and the gryphon lifted onto his back legs.

Nix flapped her blue-lavender wings and gripped the edge with her back talons. *I'm fine. Though you look a bit sick, darling.*

Vahly waved Nix's mental communication off and looked up. A cave yawned above them.

Arc leapt to grasp the black root of a skeletal pine growing from the side of the mountain, then he swung upward to land at the cave's mouth. "I'll scout it." He disappeared beyond the edge.

"What do you see?" Vahly called up, her hands shaking with cold.

Arc's face appeared at the overhang, his black hair stark against the snow gathering across his broad shoulders. "Nothing. I suggest we keep moving unless your magic says otherwise."

Snow fell in slanting sheets. Ice clung to Vahly's hair and cloak and set her teeth to chattering as Arc jumped onto Kyril's wide back and the group lifted into the sky.

Lightning broke the black clouds, and the dragons roared, enjoying the heat and flash and taking in its power. Vahly scowled at the sky and gripped Kyril's ruff to keep from falling. Arc's hand spread against her spine, and his healing magic soothed her chilled body, thawing her enough that she might be able to keep her teeth after this was all over.

Kyril flew them over the second peak, where the wind ripped at Vahly's hair and would've torn the cloak from her back had Arc not been there. Other than a few more snow-crusted pines, the area below was devoid of life. Vahly put a hand on her ribs, focusing on the magic, feeling its direction. A dark spot halfway down the third peak made her Blackwater mark pulse.

Kyril whirled around, changing course and flying straight at the darkened area. Vahly patted his side as she squinted to see through the storm. Uneven lines of darkness showed in the continuous snowfall. Perhaps a flat area where they would be able to land? At least there, they could huddle down and wait out the storm. Maybe that was all the magic was attempting to do, to keep them safe until the snow passed.

Vahly gritted her teeth. They had no time for this. Even now, Astraea was plotting her next flood, the one that would truly end it all and kill what little was left of the land. Why was the Sea Queen waiting to finish them off? With Ryton gone, Vahly had no one to make thoughtful guesses as to what Astraea might be planning.

Ryton's stern face flashed through Vahly's memory, and a weight sat on her chest as she recalled the way he'd plunged into the fray and given all. He'd been her captor, yes, but he'd been true to his heart, protecting her when his own elemental powers asked it of him. The love he'd had for his fallen sister, Selene, had shown in his actions and his mournful eyes. Ryton had sacrificed himself for the good of the world. He wouldn't be forgotten.

A gust whipped across Vahly's face, sleet pelting and burning her cheeks, as Kyril circled and nearly smashed into the rock face. She adjusted her hold on the gryphon's ruff, but her fingers wouldn't curl tightly enough to do it properly, the joints stiff with cold.

The group fell apart, then came back together, struggling to fly to the flat area to land. Thunder crashed, echoing across the mountains and making Vahly wince. The storm snarled like an army of dragons. Shivering, Vahly looked down at the earth.

"Arc. My hands." She cursed her too-human fingers and how a simple winter storm could threaten her.

Arc poured more healing warmth into her, but then Kyril dipped harshly to the side, and Arc called out something unintelligible. His voice echoed in her head, but it was only sound and no meaning. Her body shuddered, fingers slipping from the gryphon's ruff, and her body shifted, falling.

CHAPTER 4

Vahly gasped as Arc's strong arm circled her waist to pull her to safety. With a cry of fear, Kyril dropped. The movement jerked Arc's arm away and threw both of them from Kyril's back.

Magic surging inside her chest as the wind howled and buffeted her arms and legs, she called up the ground. "Rise," she whispered, her throat frozen.

A wide column of black earth, churning as it built on itself, met her back as Arc landed on his own feet, air magic spooling around his tall form. The earth's scent slowed Vahly's racing heart and the earth's hands of churned dirt lowered her so she stood near Amona.

Impressive, Daughter, Amona said through the bond as she set her bag in the snow with her massive talons. She shook out her sapphire wings, giving them a stretch.

Arc dusted himself off, his eyes shining as he looked at Vahly and the group gathered. The dirt fell away from her, returning to its bed.

Nix transformed in a flash of bright light. She dressed quickly, then looked up, grinning, lips pink in the cold and red hair flying. "I'll never get tired of seeing you work your magic."

"You and me both." Vahly adjusted her baldric and belt. "I waited long enough for it."

The darkness on the slope turned out to be a small forest of conifers and aspens, bark in varied shades of light and dark, like elven magic. Snow weighed down the trees' boughs and muffled the group's footsteps. Wind threw handfuls of the trees' white burden onto their heads and across their shoulders as the dragons shifted into their human forms and dressed quickly.

They gathered fallen wood, and Aitor lit the pile with a blast of dragonfire, flames illuminating his scarred face and glinting off the black of his hair. Vahly used her earth magic to raise a berm around them, then reached out a hand to craft the nearby living trees into a roof and door. A twinge of heat rose in her Blackwater mark, and she let her hand fall.

"Let's use the fallen pine boughs for the roof," she said.

The group agreed, and they worked until they had a makeshift shelter with a gap for smoke to escape.

Inside the shelter, with the fire belching thick smoke, and all gathered around—except Kyril who was far too large to be housed and anyway seemed untouched by the cold—Vahly explained her feeling. "It's like the trees have a mind of their own here."

Sitting on her cloak, she tapped her sword's hilt and watched their faces.

Legs crossed, Arc rested his arms on his knees and leaned forward. The fire danced in his dark eyes as he laced his long fingers. "They're older than they appear. Or at least, one has existed since the continent's creation." He cocked his head like he was listening to the wind, but then he frowned. "The wind is different here as well. It won't speak to elves."

Amona growled quietly. "Unsettling." Her bright eyes glowed in the firelight, and her sapphire scales glittered.

Aitor tore a length of dried beef, then held the second half out to Nix. "I always thought that wind thing was too strange anyway," he muttered.

Nix smacked Aitor for bad manners, then accepted the food. "Hush, fool. The elf is a king now."

The corner of Arc's mouth lifted as the wind howled outside the shelter.

Vahly took a drink from a full skin. She'd expected water, but the dizzying punch of strong cider crossed her tongue, and her head felt less surely attached to her shoulders. "I wish Kyril could be in here with us. And who brought wine?"

Nix's eyebrow lifted as she grinned. "You need to ask? What's a horrible journey into the unknown without a bit of drink?"

Aitor lifted his own wineskin to Nix, then drank deeply.

When the rations for the day were gone, the group settled as best they could to wait out the storm.

Kyril groaned outside the shelter wall, so Vahly leaned out of the doorway. The wind was dying down, and the snow fell in large clumps to gather in heaps around the gryphon. Ice crusted Kyril's feathers. He shook his snow-matted fur, his liquid eyes pinching her heart.

She raised a hand to him. "I'll be right back."

Inside, Nix poked at the fire and whispered something to Amona and Aitor. Arc studied his hand like maybe it had been injured.

Vahly nudged him. "You all right?"

He nodded, but his lips made a tight line.

"The storm let up," she said. "Kyril needs you. He's a mess."

"Of course." Arc followed her to Kyril.

Once Arc had spun his air magic to heat and dry the gryphon's massive body, the gryphon shook, then licked Arc with his spear-thin eagle tongue.

Chuckling, Nix opened her mouth, but Vahly gripped her arm. "Nix, I can imagine the ribbing you're about to give Arc. Maybe don't. If the others weren't here, it'd be fine, but they need to see him as a king. You seem to be very good at reminding Aitor of that fact, but you fail to remember it yourself."

Barking a laugh, Nix patted her hand. "All right. I'll behave," she whispered. "But you should know it's killing me not to capitalize on this Master of Fur and Feather Styling situation."

Vahly fought a laugh despite the cold that ate at her exposed skin. She shoved Nix gently, then went to stand by Arc. "Thank you for caring for him."

Arc's gaze moved from Kyril's shuffling wings to Vahly's face. He studied her as his hand went to her face and his magic curled into her, warm and welcome. She found herself sighing but coughed to cover the sound. Arc leaned closer and pressed a kiss to her lips, his crown flickering at the edges of Vahly's vision. Her body lit up like a torch at his touch, at the nearness of his body, at the feeling of his magically powerful presence.

With a jolt, her magic pulsed beneath her heart and tugged her attention away from him, toward the dark trees beyond the shelter.

Arc's gaze followed hers, and he squeezed her hand once. "Go, follow your instinct, Vahly."

A shiver went through her. "Please keep using my name."

"I will unless we're before a gathered crowd who must remember your rank." His words, though serious, held amusement.

She nodded, smiling, then started toward the tall, spindly evergreens and the darkness that beckoned.

CHAPTER 5

Her magic surged, and she moved faster, wanting to be in the midst of the trees. Murmured questions from the group carried on a gust of wind, but she ignored them. She had to get into the wood and see what her earth magic had in store.

The snow-weighted branches creaked and sifted snow onto her head as she crossed the slick ground. Flakes gathered against her boots and in her hair as she passed a half-circle of stones that reminded her of the Blackwater spring in Illumahrah. In shadows that clung to her like wet cloth, she shook out her cloak's hood and tugged it on. A trickle of freezing water snaked down the back of her neck.

Movement in the trees stopped her. Something shifted the branches behind her. She risked a glance over her shoulder to find Arc at the line of trees. She turned back around, and one of the tallest of the slim evergreens stepped forward.

Her heart shivered like the cold had broken through her very body.

The tree's broken top—devoid of green needles—seemed to scratch the snow cloud that billowed above the small forest. Two knots blinked like eyes, and a hollow worked like a mouth. Though she'd controlled much of the earth, she'd never seen anything like this. The tree had a few needled boughs, two of which seemed to serve as arms.

"Earth Queen." The creature's voice held the sounds of bending branches and wind-tossed leaves.

When she'd met the Spirit of the River, Arc had advised her to kneel. She did so now, in front of this, what had to be another spirit.

"I'm sorry if we disturbed you," she said, lifting her voice to carry to its faraway head, "but I believe my magic led me to you." The wind whistled in her ears, and she fisted her freezing hands.

"I am the Mountain Spirit, and I have a gift for you." The spirit bent low, then reached out a hand of twigs and pine needles. The woody hand uncurled to show a sprig of pine, a piece of its own body. A clutch of fresh needles sprouted from the very end.

Vahly accepted it with gentle fingers, the same fingers she'd used to steal from Lapis who taunted her as a child, to roll bones and dice for hours at the ciderhouse, to touch the Blackwater at the Source's spring, to raise the earth to protect her friends.

"Thank you. The Spirit of the River also gave me a

gift." She felt for the river stone that Arc and Nix both had cared for now and again throughout their quest. The rock's smooth surface was warm inside the deep pocket of her trousers. She showed it to the Mountain Spirit.

"Ah," the tree said. "Very good."

"What am I to do with these gifts?"

The Mountain Spirit blinked and glanced beyond Vahly, perhaps at Arc. "I know not. But you will discover your fate."

Vahly swallowed. "Can you tell if that fate will be good or bad?"

"No one can. Except perhaps the Watcher."

"Who is the Watcher?"

"Under the sea, she bides and works." The spirit turned to depart, his back looking like nothing more than a dying pine, but his presence heavy in a way that echoed the feel of Arc's ancient power.

Standing, Vahly tucked the pine twig into her pocket beside the river rock. "Thank you."

She expected the spirit to turn back toward her and say something, but the tree had gone wholly still, and her magic no longer pulled in the spirit's direction. Stepping over a fallen branch, she walked to the front of the tree. Its knot eyes had faded into the grain of the trunk, and the hollow that had served as its mouth was dark and empty.

Wind pushed at her back, and her magic hummed inside her, insistent. She had to leave now for the Sacred Oak.

Wasting no time, she ran to Arc and showed him what the spirit had given her.

Arc touched the twig with just one finger, careful not to disturb the needles, like they were younglings sleeping. "Amazing. You are the first to call up the Mountain Spirit since the time before written history." His smile warmed her. "This is a very good sign, Vahly."

She pocketed the pine sprig and strode toward Kyril, Nix, Aitor, and Amona. "From your lips to the Source's waters, elf," she said quietly, just for him, receiving a good-natured chuckle from him. "It's time, everyone," she said to the group. "I have two gifts from spirits now, and my magic is telling me we need to leave now for Illumahrah, and may the Blackwater bless our journey."

As Vahly filled them in on what had happened in the wood, the group rose into the wintry sky, heading for the blue expanse that mirrored the flooded land. Vahly kept her focus on the sea and every uneven swell that might mean an attack. Arc pressed a hand to Kyril's side, near Vahly's leg, urging the gryphon to fly quickly.

"Soon," Vahly whispered to her unseen enemy. "Soon, I will have the power to crush you, Astraea. Don't think I'll be merciful."

CHAPTER 6

The water stretched from where the sun rose over the toothlike remains of the Lapis mountain palace—a jagged line in the distance—to where the sun set over the drowned western mountains. In Vahly's nightmares, Astraea flooded the land over and over again.

Eyes watering at the sparkling sea, she shook her head. No need to borrow horror. There was plenty enough to fill her thoughts. The Forest of Illumahrah was a long way off, and she had to stay focused on the goal.

Sweat from Kyril's pelt dampened Vahly's hands as she adjusted her grip on his ruff. The gryphon's head lurched with every wingbeat, and his sides blew like bellows that might have a hole.

Arc leaned into Vahly. "Kyril will need a rest soon, hmm?"

"Exactly what I was thinking."

Flying beside them in full dragon form, Amona soared straight, eyes narrowed. Beyond her, Aitor and Nix flew in their human forms, their smaller wings working only when the wind currents didn't oblige them. They were all three flying smart, using the air in their own unique ways, but still, they hadn't revived their fire magic since the lightning storm, and the quiet between Nix and Aitor meant they were tiring as much as Kyril.

Not a speck of land jutted from the waves. Gritting her teeth, Vahly stretched her back and moved her neck to ease the stiffness that came with being in one position for so long. Arc's strong fingers massaged the tight muscles around her shoulder blades, and she sighed, pressing into him and relishing the feel of his powerful presence and his warm body against hers.

He tucked her braid over her shoulder. "I comprehend your motive to reserve your magical strength, but you underestimate yourself. You don't need land above water to work. You are the earth's master." His fingers moved across her shoulder, his skin luminous in the sunlight.

"If it turns out I don't have the power to raise enough land to a level sufficient to avoid the creatures lurking below, we're all dead."

Arc rubbed her arm and set his lips against her ear. Goosebumps rose along her neck. "Please, just attempt the task," he said. "You can do this." Arc leaned over, his sharp elven gaze on the gryphon's feathered head. "What do you think, Kyril?"

Kyril squawked.

"That sounded like a *Yes* to me," Nix called out.

Vahly grinned. Nix and Kyril had spent a good deal of time together when Vahly had been trapped with Astraea beneath the sea. They'd searched Illumahrah and brought Rigel, Haldus, and Ursae safely from the wreckage of the elven kingdom. Nix pretended not to care much about Kyril, but the warmth in her eyes that showed when she looked at him displayed the opposite.

Vahly touched Arc's knee. "If you're sure you want to risk it... Amona, what do you say? Should I try to raise land high enough for safety here in the wide-open sea?"

Giving her massive lapis-blue wings a quick flap before coasting again, Amona nodded. *We have no other choice, Daughter. And I too believe in your power.*

Vahly pushed her sleeves over her elbows then quickly grabbed hold of Kyril again. "Kyril, please circle this area." It was as good as any.

He tipped and began to turn, the sun-touched waves sparkling like broken glass far below them.

The earth's heartbeat echoed faintly, a match to the rhythm of Vahly's pulse. "Amona, when I give you the signal, breathe fire, please."

Amona circled in a wider path, encompassing Kyril's route. Nix and Aitor hovered above.

Arc's arms moved behind Vahly, and his air magic,

both light and dark, spilled from his hands to ride the air alongside them, ready.

The earth's heartbeat drummed inside Vahly's chest, racing through her blood and warming the center of her forehead, palms, and stomach. The earth waited, trembling under the seawater, wanting to rise to meet her, to obey her command. The scent of it pushed through the ocean, impossibly strong. She opened her mouth, then shut it again. Magic tugged at her chest.

"Now!" she shouted.

Arc forced his magic onto the water's chaotic surface, and Amona blasted the same spot with dragonfire. The scent of sage, sandalwood, and sun-warmed ground permeated the air. Vahly flipped her palms upward as Kyril veered around. The salt water spun away from the combined air and fire magic from Arc and Amona. At last, a circle of land showed itself. Muscles tightening in her neck and forearms, the magic coiling inside her, Vahly curled her fingers, then splayed them wide.

The ground erupted from the waves.

Kyril flew high above the rising mound that had once been part of the Jade territory boundary.

Amona circled the growing island of magically dry ground, flying expertly—sharp turns of the tips of her wings, quick flutters of just the front section, careful angling of the entire wing—studying Vahly's work as if checking it for signs of the sea kynd.

When there was a flat stretch large enough for landing, Vahly squeezed her thighs, signaling to Kyril.

They dropped down beside Amona, who reared up and blew dragonfire into the daylight, the heat warping the air around her slitted eyes. Nix and Aitor joined in.

Vahly and Arc slid off Kyril's back as he roared. Vahly winced, ears ringing.

"Take it easy, gryphon." She patted his side. "You'll deafen us all."

Amona raised her scaled eyebrows at Kyril, who now stood taller than Amona. Nix and Aitor were laughing about the roar, doing their best to mimic the strength of Kyril's lungs, and the scene reminded Vahly of nights at Nix's ciderhouse back when their friends were alive and the worst they had to worry about was a tavern brawl. Vahly's chest ached.

The surrounding water settled, lapping at the new land gently, but every wave looked like a shark's fin or a sea kynd's head clearing the surface.

"Maybe we should be a touch quieter," Vahly suggested, although she was fairly certain the cacophony of the waves covered all noise.

Aitor laughed. "Allow us a little celebration. We are a fourth of the way there, by all estimations."

Amona sat back on her haunches and stared in the direction of the ruined Lapis palace. She didn't seem inclined to shift into human form for conversation, so Vahly let her be.

Vahly gave Aitor a smile. "I suppose we should enjoy the successes when they come." She looped her arm in Arc's and joined the group's circle.

Nix pulled a pair of dice from her pocket. "Who's up for a game?"

Vahly accepted the dice from Nix and rolled them on the rough ground. "I call sevens."

It was her lucky number, and she was betting it all.

CHAPTER 7

At the edge of the newly formed island, Arc lifted his hand and turned it over, watching for what he had seen off and on during the last two days. And there it was. The flesh at the end of his fingers and on his wrist glimmered like the sea in the moonlight. An orange cast lined the borders of the strange markings, fluctuations that came and went with no apparent reason.

Spelled salt water didn't injure elves. He hadn't run into any poisonous plants of late. How could he when they'd been in the North where so little grew? His mind listed off the various curses he'd studied in scrolls and in his lab in Illumahrah. Nothing fit.

As King of the Elves, he was the most powerful of the healers. If he couldn't heal himself, no one could.

Trying again, he imagined a cool breeze sliding through his bones and blood, a spring's refreshing gust. He mentally pushed the imaginary healing to his afflicted hand, visualizing the discolored flesh and interior damage returning to a healthy glow. Gathering the magic of his elven crown, he fed the power into the healing process, but as soon as the imagined gust of magic hit the edge of his cursed hand, it fell away, dissolving.

His shoulders slumped, and he exhaled, wishing he had access to the scrolls, scrolls that were forever ruined beneath the ocean. None of the scrolls he'd read mentioned anything about a sickness such as this. Except for the orange hue here and there, the affliction wasn't too visually different from the color of dragon flesh affected by spelled salt water. But the way the condition came and went...

He shoved his hands through his hair. Rigel and Haldus might have known what to do. He should've asked about this before leaving. Instead, he'd stubbornly hoped the condition would fade, that it was some lingering magic from earlier battles with the sea folk. Perhaps a few of the sea kynd had tipped their coral spears with a venom previously unseen during their interactions.

Arc scanned the expanse of land, hoping to spot a medicinal plant that might be tried against this condition. Aside from a cluster of stunted scrub pines miraculously healthy despite their time underwater, the land was bare.

Kyril loped to his side and sat back on his haunches. The gryphon's head blocked out the sun, creating a pleasant spot of shade. Arc set his hand against the gryphon, and the creature twisted its head, eyes focusing on Arc's diseased—or cursed—hand. Kyril stretched his neck as if he were going to examine the area.

Arc pulled away. "Let it be. We have enough to worry about without fretting over a few elven fingers."

The gryphon nudged his head lovingly before trotting off to join the group.

Arc remained, looking over the edge of the new island. Salt water churned below, far enough away to protect them from sharks or other such water beasts, but the distance would be nothing to a sea kynd. If Arc and the rest of them were discovered, it would be a slaughter. Perhaps he could concoct a defense to thwart attack and raise an alarm if any disturbed the area.

Closing his eyes, he expanded his senses. The wind pushed this way and that, its haunting voice whispering about arguments fought in the distant past and calling his name in its particular fashion. The wind's essence, cool against his mind and full of information, showed his mind possibilities based on history.

When he, Vahly, and Nix had fought the old elven king, the evil Mattin, the old king had used air magic to create a wall of darkness. Those against Mattin had thrashed against the slightly transparent clouds of gray, unable to reach the evil king or to help during the fighting. The barrier had been horrifying, but perhaps such an air spellwork could be used for good?

Arc pictured the wall that the old King Mattin had

created, its cloudy depths, its sticky strength. Magic twisted inside Arc like a creature that longed to be free. He opened his eyes and extended his fingers. Dark gray magic curled away from his hands to form a wall all along the island. Lines of heat and a deep ache burst across Arc's forehead and through the afflicted hand. Gasping, he went down on one knee.

Vahly ran to him. "What's wrong? And what is this?" Her gaze traveled the perimeter.

"It's for our protection. From the sea." He coughed and got to his feet with Vahly's help, feeling foolish and hiding his affected hand in the folds of his cloak.

"What's wrong? Are you hurting because you created this?"

"I'm fine," he lied. His stomach turned and his knees felt weak, as if something sapped his strength. But he didn't think it had anything to do with this magic because the spellwork hadn't felt evil in and of itself. He had been wrong before though, and perhaps he was again.

Vahly rubbed his back. "Are you sure you're all right?"

"Yes." He touched her soft cheek.

A smile stretched her rosy lips, and he grinned.

"I don't believe you, elf," she said. "You're just being brave again and keeping secrets as you elves love to do. Don't think I'm letting this go forever."

"Come." Arc took her arm. His body warmed at her closeness, at the fresh, green scent of her magic-touched skin. Her lips truly looked ripe as berries, and his own mouth parted as he imagined a day when they could be finished with war and grief and simply enjoy one another. "Let's rest. The wall will alert us if anything attempts to attack."

Vahly grumbled but came along. She looked beautiful when she was grouchy.

The group rested and ate, talking and playing dice and doing their best to ignore the dangers literally all around them. He asked Nix and Vahly to teach him a new dice game, and he laughed in all the right places as he won every imaginary coin they put out to bet.

But the strange affliction stained every moment.

CHAPTER 8

Wind howled and blew Vahly's hair out of her face. Rubbing her sleep-puffy eyes, she jumped to her feet to see everyone else doing the same. Night had wrapped the world in black, and they'd all fallen asleep exhausted.

"What is that horrible sound?" Nix asked.

"My air magic ward," Arc said.

Vahly squinted. A light bobbed over the choppy waves, bright in the weak starlight.

"That's not the light of dragonfire from a distance, is it?" Arc asked.

"No." The rhythm of her pulse grew increasingly erratic as the strange, round light floated ever closer. "I don't think so."

The water exploded.

Three tentacles rose into the air, towering above everyone, even Kyril.

Her heart hung useless in her chest, her fingers going numb.

A creature blinked its three eyes and opened a wolf-like snout to snarl, a sound like hundreds of trees cracking in a storm. One tentacle smashed into Arc's wall of dark magic. The creature had a mouth the size of a full-grown dragon and three rows of teeth, the smallest of which was larger than Vahly's fist.

Amona spoke into her head. *The air magic will only hold him for a few moments more. I have seen this beast before. And I don't believe that wall will keep him away. We must fight it. They are a bloodthirsty kynd, always hungry.*

Vahly answered aloud. "You lived through the attack, so you know something about it." The cacophony of the creature's screeching and the sound of its tentacles battering Arc's barrier grew louder with every moment. "What are its weak spots?"

The creature's head rose then thrust to the side as a barbed fourth tentacle speared through the water and into the air.

"What in the Blackwater is that?" Aitor asked.

"It's the creature's tail," Arc said. "I've seen a drawing of this beast in an old scroll. The tail is tipped in a spine that holds a venom that paralyzes on contact."

"Delightful," Nix said before disrobing and changing into her full dragon form.

Vahly, Amona said inside her mind, *we must go for its lead tentacle. That is where its three hearts lie.*

"How do we know which one is the lead tentacle?"

Slicked in moonlight, the creature thrashed against the wall of gray-black air magic, and a flash of blood-red blinked through the chaos.

"There!" Arc pointed. "Aim for that tentacle."

"Yes!" Vahly shouted. "Amona has seen this creature before and she agrees. I'll distract it by raising myself up on a new peak. The rest of you fly around the creature and hit that blood-red tentacle with everything you've got. Kyril, go with them and strike out with your claws when you see the opportunity. Try to drive the creature toward the dragons' fire."

Kyril shrieked, obviously unhappy with the plan to leave Vahly, but he rose into the air seemingly prepared to follow her orders.

Arc was spinning more dark magic into his wall, trying to hold the sea creature back while Vahly called up the earth under her feet, the dirt trembling through her boots.

Arc called out, fell back. The barrier of air magic exploded in an array of sparkling black crystal and stars golden with power.

A tentacle lashed out at Arc and snared his foot, lifting him into the air. Vahly's throat closed as she poured her magic into the earth. She couldn't lose him. The ground rose under her until she was on level with where the beast held Arc above its great, horrible mouth.

"Kyril!" she shouted, throat raw.

The gryphon tore through the sky, and she leapt onto his back, holding her breath, praying to the Source that

Arc would survive this. She inhaled the scent of the newly turned earth that she'd pulled above the oceans and commanded the scrub pines to rise up.

All five of the small trees withdrew into the ground, then burst back from the earth in the shape of gryphons with vines for tails and roots that formed wings that spread as they soared into the air to join her and Kyril.

Magic like sunlight spun around Arc's hands, stronger on his left than on his right. Wind roared around him, lifting him and pulling him away from the sea creature. He was using his air magic to try to escape.

"Attack!" she shouted at the scrub pine gryphons.

The earth creatures snared the sea beast's head with pliable wings that then became bindings, tightening around the creature's three eyes.

All of the dragons released blasts of fire that rippled and smoked against the beast's body and tail.

The shimmering, fish-scale tail thrashed like a great snake, escaping the fire, while its venomous spike narrowly missed Aitor's scarred face. Nix, a blur of lighter blue against the night sky, zipped into the space between the creature's head and the tentacle that held Arc still. She unleashed rippling orange dragonfire along the sinuous limb, and the creature released its hold on Arc.

Eyes closed, face gray, he fell into the sea.

CHAPTER 9

Arc's eyes flashed open, and water pushed against his chest. He willed his magic to force the liquid from his lungs and spread his arms to spin a globe of protection, sourcing air from within the water to breathe. Pulling in his fill of air, he shook his head. The magic had come so easily. He kicked his feet, driving toward the surface so he could rejoin the fight against the sea beast.

Shapes swam past, a dozen or more, and he didn't have time to react before they were throwing spelled coral spears at the beast. Dashing through the red fingers of blood twisting through the currents from the sea creature's wounds, Arc hurried to join these unlikely allies. The water sizzled with sea magic as the sea kynd circled the beast, throwing their spears in turn and retrieving them with a word. Their voices thundered through the current in a way that made Arc's ears ache.

Blood darkened the battleground, and he drove toward the surface.

The beast lurched, and blood blackened the water, completely cloaking the glow of the moon and stars. Arc broke the surface, called up a wind, and leapt onto the land.

Vahly and Kyril flew close, Vahly holding out a hand for him to grab. She looked like a true goddess with her flaxen hair blowing in the wind and the way her eyes loosed arrows of fire into his heart.

Source save him, he would do anything for this female.

He grabbed Vahly's hand and jumped behind her onto the gryphon. "The sea folk are helping us defeat it."

"Yes, but why?" Vahly lifted a hand, fisted it.

The pine gryphons released the bleeding sea creature from their vines. Two coral spears jutted from the beast's torso. A female sea kynd blasted through the waves, body rising on a crest of salt water as she threw a spear at the red tentacle. The dragons and the earth gryphons blew fire, citrine and emerald, at the creature's face.

The spear hit its mark, and the sea beast roared.

The creature crashed backward into the ocean, separating the waters and sending walls of foaming spray to either side. The dragons soared high to avoid the water, but the waves caught the earth gryphons and pulled them under. They disintegrated into leaves and broken tree limbs before disappearing into the sea.

When the water calmed, everyone remained high in the air, afraid of the sea folk and their spelled salt water. But Arc noticed the female who had struck the killing blow, bobbing at the edge of Vahly's new island.

He pointed her out, his mind recalling how Vahly had looked when she'd been one of the sea kynd, how her second eyelid had blinked across her vivid irises, how her flesh had been both beautiful and incredibly foreign. He was wholly glad to have her true self back again.

"The leader of their group wishes to speak to us," he said. "We should risk it. They could have allowed that creature to kill us or at least slay me while I was underwater. I couldn't have fought off that many."

"All right. Let's give it a go." Astride Kyril, Vahly's legs shifted against Arc's, her movements giving the gryphon the request to drop from the sky to land.

Are you certain this is wise? Amona asked the group telepathically, her matriarch voice booming with power that would have made Arc wish to go to his knees before he'd taken the elven crown.

Nix joined in. *I don't trust this. They might have saved you just to bring you to Astraea. We should give them a nice little wave of thanks, then move on.*

Arc pursed his lips. *I'll remain by Vahly's side, Kyril too. If there is any sign of danger, I will blow them backward and Kyril will take our Earth Queen into the sky.*

I think Arc is right, Vahly said. *Allowing that freakish beast to slay us would've pleased Astraea just fine. This group might be like Ryton, trapped in a scenario and trying to do their best.*

Fine, Nix said. *But if the sea kynd even so much as flaps a finned finger at you, Queenie, I'm blasting the Source life right out of her tail.*

Sea folk don't have tails, Nix, Vahly said, smirking.

Not the point, darling.

Arc summoned his air magic, keeping it at the ready as he trailed Vahly and Kyril to the water's edge.

The sea kynd female raised her eyes, squinting like the light caused pain as she watched the dragons. Her face showed the scars of battle. A jagged line marred her left cheek and mangled one of her gills, and shining flesh showed where hair should have been above her ear, a slash that would've killed a lesser being.

"Can you speak to us?" Vahly asked.

Earth power vibrated from her words, and Arc was fairly certain she wasn't fully aware of the effects her magical abilities had on those around her. She was far too humble.

The sea kynd female held her webbed fingers toward Arc, raising her eyebrows, then she lowered her hands into the water. "Here," she said, her voice a rasping croak, barely intelligible.

Vahly glanced at Arc, her lips turning up at one side. "You up for another swim, King Arcturus?"

He bowed. "If it pleases you, my queen."

Normally, these words would've drawn an impish

grin across Vahly's lovely face, but now a wariness cloaked her feigned nonchalance.

The sea kynd female moved back as he lowered himself into the water. The surface had thankfully calmed since the demise of the sea beast. The tides were strong, tugging at his legs, but he was glad for them because they had obviously drawn the dead sea creature away.

The female sea kynd's tentative eyes relieved some of his hesitation; something about her urged him to trust her.

Before he went fully under, Vahly gripped his hand, her gaze going to his discolored fingers. She lifted her eyebrows at him, but then blinked and clicked her tongue like she was thinking there was a better time to ask him about his affliction.

"You're certain you want to do this?" she asked.

"I am." He gave her an encouraging nod, then submerged beneath the water.

CHAPTER 10

A rc forced himself to move slowly, carefully. Under the water, the female sea kynd and her fellows gathered around him in a loose formation. He spun a globe of air magic around himself so he could breathe but kept the magic woven loosely so speech could carry more easily.

"Greetings. I am King Arcturus. Thank you for your help in fighting off the sea beast."

Several large males with beards of black, sea-green, and silver swam nearby, their coral spears now back in their hands due to their specific spell work, a magic he'd witnessed when helping Vahly escape Tidehame. Two other females flanked the leader as well, their spears held pointed at him and their pale orange hair floating in the currents. They looked exactly alike, twins perhaps. The one to the leader's right had a second spear— perhaps their leader's weapon.

With hands spread to show she was unarmed, the

leader regarded him with serious eyes. "Greetings, King Arcturus of the Elves, destined mate to the Earth Queen. We have heard talk of you across the ocean. I am Lilia, wife of a murdered general who served Astraea. I gathered those who, like me, detest Astraea's ways. We have joined together to rebel against her." Her voice rippled through the moonlit water, the sounds jarring, making understanding her difficult. "We do not recognize her as queen. There are many more of us, rebels, who move against Astraea in an attempt to thwart her plans and give the Earth Queen the opportunity to balance the world."

"Greetings, Rebel General Lilia. Thank you for slaying the beast."

The rebels nodded once in unison.

"I must ask," he said, the salt water pinching at his throat and his magic spinning around him, delivering the sounds to Lilia's ears, "what would you like to see Queen Vahly of the Earth accomplish?"

Lilia's head turned as she gazed at the silvery water and the seaweed already growing tall on ground where dragons had so recently hunted deer and goat. "Balance. I spoke to the Watcher, and she sees a possible balance between land and sea, but it will only come to pass if every soul involved in these efforts gives their all."

"The Watcher?"

"She is our...Seer, I think you would say. General Ryton, the male who aided you, he worked with her."

The male sea kynd had fought alongside Vahly, Nix,

Kyril, and Arc when Astraea had attacked at the Lost Valley. He had sacrificed himself to save them, and Arc would never forget him.

"We believe Ryton died; is that right?" Arc asked gently. He hoped that some strange occurrence might have seen him escape. "I'm sorry for your loss if you did indeed know him. He was a brave warrior and deserving of honor."

Lilia's chest moved, and Arc couldn't help but wonder exactly how the sea folk's gills and lungs interacted. "Yes. We lost him. We heard of his death from a spy in Astraea's ranks. Ryton was a dear friend of mine, the bravest of us all, and was like a brother to my murdered husband. Before any of us had gathered ourselves enough to begin our own fight, Ryton rebelled against Astraea because of what she did to my husband, to Grystark."

"We have all lost so many. How can we work together to realize the Seer's possible future of balance and save the rest of us? Do you have ideas?"

"Astraea told one of her guards," Lilia said, "that the Earth Queen must present herself to the Sacred Oak in Illumahrah."

"It shouldn't stun me that Astraea knows every detail, but I admit, I'm surprised," he said.

Lilia's eyebrows—not too different from his own—rose. "She knows much. Too much. We'd like to escort you the rest of the way to Illumahrah. We can stay hidden and watch for Astraea's troops, spies, and also for further sea creatures who could cause trouble."

"That would be incredibly helpful. I'm certain Queen Vahly would gladly accept your assistance. What do you ask in exchange?"

"Only that she follows her magic. True earth magic should lead her to respect the balance between land and sea. We ask that she refrain from destroying all of our kynd and our home and that she remember that we too have a right to live in our own way."

"Queen Vahly has a pure soul, though she would jest and pretend she doesn't." He fought a smile that was inappropriate for such a serious meeting. He could almost see Vahly tossing a pair of dice from hand to hand and making some sort of comment about betting on his ability to make the female sea kynd forget all about the ocean. "She'll uphold the balance. I give you my word as the Elven King." He touched the magic of his crown and held out a hand.

Lilia reached out and pressed a palm against the globe of air magic. The tendrils of air magic he'd taken from his crown seeped through the sphere to curl around Lilia's shimmering fingers in a magical oath.

"Thank you, King Arcturus. One thing you must know for the upcoming battle: The Watcher told us the Sea Queen must give a portion of her blood willingly to Vahly at the right moment to balance the world. If we kill her before that, I don't know what will happen."

"Willingly." He didn't want to say it aloud, but that

seemed quite clearly impossible. "What if we end this Sea Queen's life and your folk find a new one who would be willing?"

"It could happen. But Astraea has been the only of our kynd born Touched with the mark in generations. If we choose that strategy, there could be a long wait for the next, and I don't know what to expect."

Arc tapped his chin and watched a group of sun-yellow fish zip past. "We might create an entirely new problem if we slay Astraea before the new Sea Queen is born, yes?"

"That would be my guess, though I hate to voice it. I'd see Astraea dead at the human's feet, blooded and broken, at almost any cost. Almost. I wouldn't rush the deed though if it meant the end of us all." She turned her head and studied something in the distance that Arc couldn't see. "You should depart quickly," she said. "An odd magic stirs the water."

"The Sea Queen?"

"No. Something...different. Apart. Not a kynd."

"I had best go, then. Thank you again for your help. We'll raise another resting spot this time tomorrow and will talk again if you agree."

Lilia gave a bow of her head, then spun, her finned legs silver in the watery moonlight pooling on the surface above them.

Arc quickly left the water and climbed ashore to share all with Vahly and the others.

Amona settled beside Vahly. The Lapis Matriarch

shifted into her smaller form and donned the garments she'd brought. "This is unprecedented, the way the rebels are aiding us. I'm quite hopeful."

Nix and Aitor also shifted, and everyone gathered to discuss the possibilities and to recount Ryton's sacrifice.

Nix sipped from a waterskin that smelled strongly of ale. "But if the rebels escort us to Illumahrah, won't their presence alert Astraea?"

Arc took the proffered waterskin and swallowed down a dose. "General Lilia says they'll attempt to remain unnoticed. I suppose they have their ways."

"We can't afford to deny them." Amona took the ale from him with a graceful, blue-scaled hand.

Vahly blew out a breath and ran her hands through her hair, loosing her braid. "I can't believe we won't be able to go right after Astraea and kill her. It'll be near impossible to keep her controlled but alive in a battle."

Amona's bright eyes narrowed, and she turned toward the center of the island.

A scent rose in the air, and the wind whispered to Arc, an urging in its tone, a plea to stand and pay attention.

Amona's nostrils flared. "Vahly."

Arc stood and surveyed the spit of land. The moonlight caught on a shape behind Vahly. He'd lost all his arrows during the battle, so he drew upon his magic. "A spirit approaches."

Vahly joined him, a hand on her sword and her gaze searching. "I don't see anything."

The dragons created a wall around her, wings spread slightly to protect but not to block Arc's and her view.

Arc tilted his head and studied the watery light. The shape coalesced into a male, human-like figure, stouter than Vahly, its large eyebrows bunched. But the shape wasn't fully whole or of this world. Its body remained cloudy and held the color of the moon, pale and unsubstantial.

Vahly tugged Arc's sleeve. "What is it?" she hissed, drawing her sword.

The being's scent held notes of earthblood and minerals found deep inside the land. It could only be one thing. He stepped between Vahly and the creature, his muscles coiling, his body readying for battle, magic swirling high and strong around his temples and hands.

"It's a galtzagorri, a legendary land spirit known for interacting with humans when they were abundant. He is either here to serve you or to kill you."

CHAPTER 11

Vahly leaned around Arc and squinted. With the pearly tint outline and a body that wasn't much more than mist, the creature looked like one of the human ghosts the Spirit of the River had shown her when they'd left the Lapis cave palace before their quest. He was a thick-bodied fellow with a face only a mother could love.

"You must come with me, Earth Queen," he said. "You must prove who you are before I can give you my aid."

And by the Source did she need it. They needed all the help they could get if they had any chance to defeat Queen Astraea and her rising tides. "What happens if I don't prove who I am?"

"I will fight you, and you will die"

"Lovely. Can't I simply show you who I am right now?" Vahly waved her hand, and the earth rose, answering immediately. The creature raised its eyes to her. "Doesn't that prove I am the Earth Queen?"

The galtzagorri shook its wide head. "Many of your kynd have done as much throughout the ages. You must show you are the one we have waited for to rebalance the world. It is not a test of magic. It is a test who you are. Travel under the ground to the home of the galtzagorri, where our Blackwater Source spring will judge you. You must go alone, take this risk, and prove your mettle."

Vahly placed a hand on Kyril, whose body rumbled with a quiet growl. "Well," she said, facing Arc, Nix, Amona, and Aitor, "I was accepted by the Spirit of the River and the Mountain Spirit. I suppose this third land spirit might approve of me as well. There has to be a reason why all these spirits are approaching me and giving me items. If I don't return in a day, go onto Illumahrah without me if you're willing. See if you can find the Sacred Oak." She turned toward the galtzagorri. "Do you happen to know if the Sacred Oak still stands and how we might find it?"

"It is not my place to tell you such things. You must travel that road with your band of the four kynds."

Nix rolled her bright yellow eyes. "Of course."

Vahly touched Nix's hand. "Perhaps I'll end up meeting you there instead of returning here. There's no way to know what to expect."

Nix sauntered over to the galtzagorri. "How long is this going to take? I don't appreciate the fact that you're being so vague about this mission. This is the Earth

Queen we're talking about. You can't jerk her around like you might have the humans once upon a time."

The galtzagorri glared, then clapped his ghostly hands.

Nix collapsed to the ground.

Kyril leapt at the galtzagorri, but the spirit passed through the gryphon. Vahly's stomach lurched like she'd been kicked, and her earth magic roared to life. She encased herself, Arc, and Nix in a burrow of sorts. Arc spun an orb of light, and he held it to Nix's face. Her eyes remained closed.

Vahly touched her cheek, Nix's scales soft and smooth under her fingers and a gentle pulse beating under her jaw. "She's alive. Just knocked out. I want to kill that spirit, but I'm guessing death isn't on my list of options."

Arc placed a palm on Nix's chest, near her collarbone. "His power has placed her in a deep sleep. I can't heal this. Only time will wake her, if I had to make a prediction."

Vahly jabbed her sword into the burrow's wall and shouted, expelling frustration. Her magic surged, pushing her to move onward, toward the Forest of Illumahrah but also urging her to turn toward the galtzagorri. "I'm so sick of being torn in two. I have to follow my magic though. It's helped me so far. It's the only way to go."

She spoke softly to the earth, and the burrow crumbled into small piles around them. Aitor hurried to

Nix while Vahly stepped over the remains of the dirt wall and approached the galtzagorri, who was singing something to Kyril. The gryphon's head was cocked to one side, and Amona had the bottom edge of Kyril's scruff bunched in her hand.

The galtzagorri's song tugged at Vahly's magic, pulling the invisible line hooked below her heart, the connection between her and Kyril also humming with power. This song was truly affecting her familiar. She frowned. The galtzagorri's voice was deep, and it rumbled like the beginnings of an earthquake or a landslide.

"Oh hallowed halls of coal and quartz,
Sing greetings to the one in which we hope.
The Source will judge her true or false,
All will win or all will fall,
Under the hand of the one we call."

The creature continued the tune though without words.

Vahly crossed her arms. "Spirit," she said, giving her tone a nice dose of queenly command. "Will my dragon friend wake? I won't leave until you assure me that she'll be all right."

"She will wake. She must visit a dream in which she learns to respect the land from which she was born."

Vahly and Amona exchanged glances that said how much they both doubted Nix was the type to learn anything from anyone.

"If she dies," Vahly said, stepping closer, staring into the galtzagorri's face, "I will have revenge."

"You will not. It would be impossible. Now, let us go." The galtzagorri clapped his hands, and the earth fell away, taking him and her with it.

CHAPTER 12

Vahly opened her eyes to find the galtzagorri leading her down a tunnel lit only by the pale light of his ghostly form. She had been following him, entirely unconscious. Her shirt stuck to her skin, and her hair was plastered to the back of her neck and her temples.

"Please tell me we're not actually going to trek into the molten center of the globe. I may have grown up with dragons, but I assure you, I am not one."

The spirit didn't turn around or react to her words. He just kept on striding purposefully forward as the tunnel sloped downward.

The heat grew more oppressive with every turn, and Vahly's chest tightened. She felt like she was being buried. A ridiculous fear for an Earth Queen, surely, but she felt it all the same.

Glancing back, the galtzagorri regarded her with

serious eyes. "You will not be harmed during your journey to the land spirits' Blackwater."

A shallow comfort. He said nothing about when she arrived. To battle her fear, she focused on her magic's pull, specifically the element of the power that was drawing her directly behind the galtzagorri, toward his planned destination. This was right. She was following the earth's heartbeat, seeing this through. No matter what the spirits threw at her, she was the Earth Queen. She would prove it. Countless lives had been sacrificed to give her this chance to balance the world, and she wouldn't let primal fear crush her now.

The galtzagorri glanced back again, but this time he nearly smiled. "That's much better, human."

His gaze flitted to her Blackwater mark, and she touched the circle of shimmering darkness there, wondering if he thought her Touched mark was a mistake as so many dragons had during her life.

The tunnel opened into a large hall, the walls carved roughly as if by wide talons of a dragon unlike any she'd ever met. It was a primitive sort of place with no decoration or symbols, no furniture or places set for comfort. The pearly light that made up her host expanded and dragged across the ground like a creeping fog, drawing a chill across Vahly's bones despite the suffocating heat. The fog spun and rose to create a crowd of galtzagorri that didn't look too different from her host. Some were taller, but not by much. A few appeared female in shape, with softer mouths and finer brows. They all faced her and spoke as one, her host included.

"Meet yourself in the spring, Earth Queen. Show yourself. Show the land. Earn the love of our world's heart."

Vahly swallowed. No pressure. She exhaled and started forward. The spirits parted to reveal a low well carved of the same rock as the walls and the tunnel. She leaned over the well to see Blackwater glistening inside, ruby, amethyst, jade, and sapphire flecks of light blinking from the depths. She'd thought the only pure Blackwater spring was in Illumarah. But this one was surely pure as well. It held no magma like the dragons' earthblood vents. This spring showed no signs of holding salt water like the ones under the sea surely did.

The Blackwater pulled at her so strongly that she gripped the edge of the well to keep herself from crawling in, a fascinating yet also horrifying impulse. The scent of the earth filled her nose—heated stone, damp dirt, and minerals she could almost taste in the air. A perfume rose from the Blackwater as well, that same intoxicating blend that smelled like jasmine, clean water, and a scent she could only relate to beeswax candles.

"You are Touched," her host said, his insubstantial finger drawing across her Blackwater mark. "And so you may touch." His gaze went to the spring.

Vahly nodded and dipped her hand slowly into the well. The spirits ceased all movement and seemed to hold their collective breath as Vahly's fingers broke the surface and disappeared under the shimmering, blessed liquid.

A peace—like the morning sun after a hard-won battle, like the feel of Arc's lips on her forehead, like the sound of Nix laughing, like Amona's motherly embrace —slid over Vahly's entire body, swaddling her in the knowledge that all was right with the world. She was following the magic born inside her.

She hadn't realized she'd closed her eyes, but when she opened them, she saw her face in the Blackwater. But it wasn't the face she had now. The Blackwater's gently rippling surface painted the image of Vahly as a small child, toddling beside Amona. Child Vahly held a toy in her hand, something small that sparkled under the torches they passed as they walked down the corridors of the Lapis palace. Child Vahly looked up to see another dragon scowling down, eyeing her Blackwater mark and curling his scaled lip to show his teeth. Before Vahly could see what Amona would do to protect her, one of the many moments in which her adoptive mother had defended her with cutting words and sharp commands, the memory went hazy.

A strange feeling passed through Vahly, a sensation akin to shame. The image faded completely, and then Vahly saw herself as a girl about the age of Ruda, all arms and legs. Young Vahly shouted at a group of dragons flying around the feasting hall, playing a game of chase that involved breathing dragonfire over opponents' heads. The game served as training for battle and the adults strongly encouraged playing. The dragons ignored young Vahly's shout and taunted her when they did look her way, pointing to her Blackwater mark and laughing. Young Vahly threw an obscene gesture and sauntered out of the room in a way that showed she had already met Nix. Only Nix could teach a scrappy girl how to walk like that.

Vahly's chest ached. The pain felt fresh, the dejection new and real and very present. She shook her head. Images from her memories danced across the ceiling and over the walls. The spirits watched her failures like it was some sort of sad playacting.

Vahly dragged her gaze back to the spring to see herself grown, leaving a Dragonfire ritual with shoulders sagging. Memory Vahly straightened on seeing Nix, and the two laughed their way to the ciderhouse, where they picked up a game of bones with Dramour. Grief welled in Vahly and poured through her. She reached into the Blackwater to touch the image of Dramour's eye patch. Her eyes burned, but she refused to cry. Stones, she refused to feel shamed for any of this. None of it was her doing. This was simply her journey. The fact that she'd never been fully accepted into her mother's clan had only pushed her to fight harder in their battles with the Jades, to grow courage in face of being the smallest, the weakest, the least powerful, the most disappointing. Her difficult youth had brought her to Nix, her greatest friend, and to Arc, whom she loved more than she cared to admit. Only through her tribulations had she learned how to be swift, clever, cunning, and determined. And with these learned attributes, she had found her familiar, Kyril, a beautiful beast that made her whole.

She whirled away from the Blackwater and raised her chin. "I will not bend under these difficult memories. I thank the Source for the life I've been given. Without it, I would be nothing. I would have already been dead from neglect and lack of spirit. I am Vahly, Blooded for the Battle, Earth Queen and the one fated to balance our world. I will not be thrown off course. I will rise. I will win."

The spirits erupted in clapping and joyful shouts, surrounding her and flooding her vision with their illuminated faces and hands. Her host reached through the crowd, his fisted hand held aloft. His fingers opened, and she caught a primitive-looking dagger made entirely of obsidian.

"From your people in Bihotzetik. It is not just a dagger."

She gripped it carefully, the ebony hilt smooth against her palm. "Thank you. Any ideas on how I'm supposed to use these gifts you spirits are so kindly bestowing?"

The galtzagorri just grinned and clapped his hands.

Spirits and cave walls blurring around her, Vahly was flung upward. She was going to ram straight into the ceiling. Her heart pounded as she willed herself into a trusting state. So far, the spirits had helped, not hurt. Surely, they wouldn't smash her against the inside belly of this place. Faster and faster she flew through the air, then, as she hit the rock wall, the world went dark for moment. She was bodiless, senseless…

And then her vision returned, and she was being lovingly attacked by Kyril's massive paws, slobbering tongue, and frighteningly dangerous beak.

Beyond Kyril, Nix shook her head. Arc, Aitor, and Amona gathered around as Nix stood and brushed herself off. "Where is that ugly little spirit? I have a few words to say to him."

Amona's mouth lifted at one corner, and Arc covered a grin. Aitor put an arm around Nix, who gave him a quick kiss on the cheek before slipping out of his grip.

Vahly examined the obsidian knife the galtzagorri had given her. "Thanks for waking her up," she whispered, knowing Nix hadn't fulfilled the supposed "learning" the spirit had wanted of her and Nix had most likely only been released from whatever magic was cast on her because of a favor from the galtzagorri.

She held out the knife. "Nabbed another present, folks. I say let's get on our way."

Nix lifted into the air. "Agreed. The world isn't going to save itself."

Vahly and Arc climbed onto Kyril's back, and Vahly leaned into the elf's embrace.

Arc pressed a kiss against the back of Vahly's head, then ran his fingers along the side of her neck. Shivers danced down her back. "I worried they might be less helpful than the other spirits," he whispered.

"Oh, were you going to unleash your Elven King viciousness on them? I would've liked to see that."

His laugh ruffled her hair as Kyril launched into the night sky behind Amona and Aitor. "You will see my power. All too soon, I'm sure."

But he didn't sound sure, and his hesitation chilled Vahly's heart. He was definitely dealing with something he didn't want to talk about. But she wouldn't push him. Not yet. If she needed to know, he would tell her. He wouldn't risk the quest for pride. Arc had never been one for making himself look better than he was. No, he had a reason, she was certain.

After tucking the obsidian dagger into the baldric strapped across her chest, Vahly gripped Kyril's scruff and did her best to enjoy the flight through the quiet skies. Soon enough, death would be grasping at them again.

CHAPTER 13

Imagining the way her murdered husband Grystark used to swim, Lilia kicked her finned legs and drove through the turbulent currents of the ocean. The shadows of dragons and one gryphon blocked most of the filtered moonlight as she swam with vengeance and grief as her closest companions.

Lilia would see Astraea broken for what she had done to Grystark.

At Lilia's right, Yenn swam hard, eel-blue hair flying behind her and gaze darting to watch for any of Astraea's troops or scouts.

Yenn had been one of Astraea's most promising young warriors, but Lilia had persuaded her to join the rebellion after Grystark's death. Grystark and Lilia had helped raise Yenn after she'd lost her own parents in a battle against the Jades. It wasn't easy risking Yenn like this. Lilia well knew what would happen to Yenn if she were caught here, helping the queen's enemy.

When Astraea had found Lilia and the rebels in their first meeting place, that cave where Lilia and Grystark used to meet as young lovers, Astraea and her warriors had killed all but the dozen Lilia had managed to help escape out the cave's back entrance. In the limited hours Lilia had slept since then, nightmares of those rebels' screams haunted her. Their deaths were on her hands because of her push to revolt against Astraea's insanity.

Lilia reached her webbed hands forward through the bubbling water, gripping her coral spear and whispering spells to swim faster, to keep the lead and remain beneath the flying earth kynds overhead. She shook off her guilt. No, the rebels had been committed to the cause just as she was. They had chosen to risk their lives to fight Astraea. Claiming it was her own fault only belittled their heroism. Lilia truly felt as though there was no other choice except to keep fighting Astraea as best they could even with only a dozen to do the work. Astraea's madness would ruin the world. There was no way the Source meant for things to go this way. With no land, the weather would change, or so the Watcher had told her during their clandestine meeting in her dark cave. Storms would twist the seas and uproot the sea folk's cities. Why couldn't Astraea see that? Why wouldn't she listen? She was so clearly out of her mind with the need to hold power over all. And why couldn't the rest of Astraea's warriors see the madness of the pursuit?

"Lilia. There is movement."

Lilia's heart beat faster. The blurry outline of a bulky male with long hair materialized beyond a ridge of coral and stone, and she relaxed a fraction. "It's Gracus."

The first of their two scouts swam up to meet them, matching their pace. "I spoke to Demi." Demi was the second scout, sent all the way to the base of the elven homeland to watch for Astraea's warriors or other sea folk who might be passing through. "He said a band of merchants was headed this way, passing through toward Tidehame from the oilfish hunting."

"We will need to avoid them." Lilia's mind whirled over the possibilities. The water was so open here. They could be spotted from miles away.

Yenn flipped her spear, water magic sizzling in the current, and sliced a path through a floating tangle of seaweed so Lilia could pass easily. "But if they're only merchants, they aren't involved in the war."

"They have mouths that will speak of us," Lilia said, "and minds that will wonder what we are up to in this newly flooded area. Word will get back to Astraea. We must avoid them."

Gracus looked west, his hair pooling around his head. "Too late."

They stopped, treading water. Lilia waved the rest of her rebels—a sad number of eight warriors—to continue and keep up with the Earth Queen.

Above what appeared to be the remains of a human bridge, a group of sea folk swam in an unorganized line.

Packs hung from their backs, and two held a net of shimmering oilfish between them.

"They do indeed appear to be hunters and merchants, not merely spies," Lilia said. "I'll speak to them. Gracus, you go on ahead and inform the others that we have a small issue to deal with. Tell the Earth Queen as well. We shouldn't be too long. Yenn, do you remember the spell we cast on the younglings in the village?"

Gracus sighed, then left with a quick nod of obedience.

Yenn's eyes darkened. "How could I forget?"

"We'll need to use it again on this group, I'm afraid."

"I hate this spell."

"You know I do too," Lilia said. "But it's for their safety as well as ours. We can't let Astraea know where we are and where the Earth Queen is."

Yenn sighed, bubbles rising from her mouth and scattering across a small school of grassfish swimming overhead. "Doesn't she already know? She is aware that the human mage must find the Sacred Oak."

"Astraea has been busy with her plans for the next wave. She does know where the Earth Queen is headed, but from what Demi heard when he was last spying in her ranks, Astraea believes she is still in the northern mountains. Besides that, Astraea doesn't know where exactly the Sacred Oak grows."

They swam closer to the traveling group and Lilia raised a hand. "Greetings, hunters and merchants."

Three females and two males, one barely old enough to be hunting, smiled in a friendly way despite the fatigue that showed in the lines around their eyes and the slump of their shoulders.

"Greetings," the largest male said. "I didn't realize we were in the way of a military move. Apologies. We will be on our way as quickly as possible."

Lilia knew she and Yenn had to hit these folk with the spell now before they realized what was happening. She glanced at Yenn, who nodded. "Not a problem. May I ask how the currents are shifting near the tip of the new land shelf? We're headed there next."

Blue hair swirling around her shoulders, Yenn spoke the basis for the spell.

The young male was staring at Lilia. "Eh, I think I saw a carving of you in the reports," he said, squinting at her scarred face.

"I doubt it. I'm not very high ranking." Lilia smiled and hated herself for the deceit. Never once had she lied about a single thing. But since Grystark's death...

Life was complicated, and it didn't serve the best interests of the innocent to stand on ultimate truthfulness. Not when it would end up with more good folk dead.

"No, I'm sure of it." He spun and started a question aimed at one of the females, but Yenn pointed her spear at him.

Lilia called up the spell on her own spear and shot the magic fizzing through the water at the rest of the group. Between her magic and Yenn's, they had all of them cloaked in the memory-altering casting.

But then the young male wiggled free of the vibrating water that showed the spell's boundaries. He flew from the area and shouted a name.

Steeling her heart, Lilia pointed her spear at the young male and blasted him with power. His body went limp, and his eyes shuttered as he floated into a forest of seaweed.

Yenn finished Lilia's part of the spell, the portion Lilia had to cease chanting in order to deal with the male, then Yenn swam over to help Lilia tie the male to a drowned land tree.

"Is he..." Yenn grimaced at the youth's soft cheeks.

"No. He will live. But we must move this group on without him. Hopefully, by the time this magic-resistant fellow wakes, they'll be long gone. Knocking him out and keeping him hidden should give us a day at least."

"We need more than a day," Yenn said quietly.

Lilia gritted her teeth. "I'm not going to kill him." She remembered the blood in the water at the cave when Astraea had attacked. "Not like this."

"You might be killing us by saving him."

"It's a risk we're taking. Do you agree?"

Yenn studied Lilia's face, and Lilia felt the gaze like a press of a finger. "All right. Agreed. But we must tell the others the risk is now higher."

Lilia clapped a hand on the back of the leader, the big male, then she pointed away from the younger male they'd had to temporarily immobilize. "I heard a great school of rockgills were seen just beyond that reef there."

The man blinked and waved his group to begin heading in that direction. "Rockgills?"

"Yes. The dark-finned ones. Best tasting, in my opinion."

"Of course they're the best tasting. We'll make our year's wage on that alone. Come!" The group swam away quickly, leaving the young male in the dim shadows of the seaweed.

Lilia led Yenn back to their original route, and soon they were speeding into the dark water toward the former plateau of the elven homeland.

She would tell the other rebels and Queen Vahly too, but it was hardly riskier. The entire venture was already the most dangerous idea in the wide, watery world.

CHAPTER 14

Wind swept across the flooded Red Meadow and raked Vahly's cheeks. She tasted salt on her tongue, and her eyes were dry from trying to see over the sun-splashed water. A slip of darkness showed in the distance.

"We're here," she said, her voice carrying back to Arc, who rode behind her on Kyril. "Illumahrah." She tensed, knowing this would be a difficult moment for Arc, to say the least.

They flew above what had once been thick forests of pine and oak, beech and maple. Waves churned where the once luxurious tree palace had stood—a palace that should have been Arc's since he'd claimed the elven crown. Vahly imagined all those scrolls with ancient information lost to the sea, ripped and soaked and ruined alongside the kynd who had written them. Astraea had flooded Illumahrah, the home of the elves, when Vahly had been trapped under the water. Time had passed so that the bodies of Arc's kynd had returned to the earth naturally, but the pall of death still hung over the realm. Clouds gathered overhead as if the very sky mourned the loss of such a powerful, knowledgeable, and peaceful kynd.

A mist swirled up from the surface of the water to spray Vahly's face. Kyril shook his feathered head and scattered more drops over Vahly and Arc.

Vahly squeezed Arc's knee gently. There were no words that would be good enough. He knew she cared and she mourned with him. The touch and their growing bond felt strong, and she knew he had to feel it too. Now more than ever, she longed to be truly bonded with him, to seal their joined fate for better or worse. She wanted to feel his body next to hers, to breathe his breath, her heart beating against his in a shared rhythm. But such a bonding would have to wait until she fought Astraea. There was no time for the joys of love just yet. Perhaps there never would be. But Vahly could hope, and by the Source, she would hope with everything in her.

"Queen Vahly!" Nix flew forward and jerked her chin toward the center of the now flooded plateau. "I see land."

"Impossible." The whole place was under water. How in the world was she supposed to find the Sacred Oak under the sea?

"Yes," Arc said, his voice tight with unspoken

emotion. "The circle is protected somehow." The awe in his tone said he hadn't known about this.

And then Vahly saw the land for herself. Though swamped with a heavy fog, the dry area formed a perfect circle amid the choppy salt water, and lording over it all stood a towering oak with long, gnarled limbs, leaves wine-dark from the season's turn. The scent of earth, the scent of her own magic, spooled from the Sacred Oak like thick incense, piercing the metallic odor of the mist and the salt of the ocean.

Her magic drummed through her. Yes, it seemed to say. Now. The earth's heartbeat echoed her own, stronger and louder in her chest and her ears as they neared. Power surged inside her veins, filling her with a pleasant heat and the desire to take Astraea on right this very moment.

Heart rising with a burning hope, Vahly used her legs and feet to urge Kyril into a slow, winding path down to the circle. Through her connection with Kyril, she could feel his worry. Telepathically, the gryphon showed her the image of the Sacred Oak again, as he had when they were still in the northern mountains. In his image, yellow flowers bloomed around the oak's wide base as if it were spring. She saw what she guessed were Kyril's parents in this memory passed down through the gryphon's special kind of magic. His father had been darker in feather color and thicker around the neck than Kyril. Kyril's mother had possessed a glossy pelt. In the image, her fur reflected a long-ago sunbeam.

They were majestic, just as Kyril was, and Vahly told him as much, bending over his neck to whisper to him as they landed.

They settled among the rest of the party a good distance from the Sacred Oak, which hid in the mist like a dream.

The dragons remained in their human forms, split cloaks wrinkled and the hems—sewn with the Jade symbols—on their borrowed shirts, dresses, and Aitor's trousers dirty. The fabric clung to their scaled blue bodies, the mist still blanketing the area.

Vahly slid from Kyril's back and turned to check on Arc. His dark eyes were shadowed, the ink and gold light of his crown just barely visible when Vahly focused instead on Arc's parted lips.

"I am home," he said quietly, his voice a deep rumble and filled with power. He lifted his chin and regarded the oak. "I feel this place welcoming me."

As his presence rolled over Vahly—intoxicating, invigorating—he inhaled, eyes closing as the wind lifted the ends of his straight black hair and the edges of his cloak. Her lips longed to find his and feel his power wash through her, to join her magic with that of an elven king, a soul she had grown to love as much as her own.

Nix straightened her borrowed dress, then bent to pick a sprig of fall berries from a low bush. She tucked the tiny berries and their emerald leaves behind one ear. Her red hair hung damp over one shoulder as she winked at Vahly.

"Time to show us the goods, Queenie. Let's see that earth magic rise."

Vahly almost laughed. Even the worst of situations couldn't keep Nix's humor down for long. "Glad you're taking time to get pretty for a tree."

"It can't hurt to look one's best when dealing with the one magical living thing to survive through a historic, catastrophic flood." Nix started up the sloping hill, hitching her skirts and raising an eyebrow. "That tree isn't just a tree."

Amona and Aitor trailed Nix, Vahly, and Arc, with Kyril following. The mist occasionally broke open to show the sun overhead and the Sacred Oak beyond their path of tall, waving grasses and patches of sage, lavender, and hyssop.

Vahly's magic bloomed inside her, growing strong against her ribs, spreading through her blood. Her fingers and Blackwater mark tingled, excitement coursing through her bones.

The oak's farthest-reaching roots, slightly exposed here and there in the mossy ground, appeared at Vahly's feet.

Feeling joined to the ground beneath her, she dropped to a knee and bowed her head. Tears sprang to her eyes, but she willed them back. They weren't tears of sadness but of joy. She knew, without a doubt, she was in the place she had been meant to be since her birth.

CHAPTER 15

The leaves of the Sacred Oak shuffled in the autumn wind that blew over Vahly and Kyril. The others stayed back as the voices of Vahly's ancestors whispered in the scratch of branches rubbing together and the clatter of acorn bunches thick in the boughs high above this holy ground. Vahly stopped, a hand on Kyril's side, the sudden urge to remove her boots overwhelming. She unlaced them, slid her stockings free, then walked with Kyril across the cool grass and rough roots that warmed at the touch of toe and heel.

At the trunk of the tree, Vahly set her forehead, her Blackwater mark, against the deeply ridged grain. The earth's heartbeat drummed in her palms, and she felt the strength of Kyril feeding her, his warmth helping her reach into the Sacred Oak with her magic. She felt as though her feet were the tree's roots. Her toes stretching through the dirt, rock, and earthblood far below.

Nothing could move her. She could stand here for eternity and live well, quiet and strong. But the image of Nix's grin, Arc's eyes, and Amona's tears singed her mind, and she slowly pulled back.

In the wood, the outline of a sword glittered like polished gems.

Three hollows appeared around the sword's shape. Kyril sent an image to Vahly's mind. She saw the Spirit of the River's stone, the Mountain Spirit's pine sprig, and the galtzagorri's obsidian dagger.

Vahly smiled at him and removed the three items from her pockets. The dagger was warm to the touch, the river stone cool as a stream, and the bit of pine nearly frozen. Not quite sure how to go about this, Vahly set the dagger into the hollow as if the place were meant to be a shelf for the weapon.

The tree creaked as if it were about to lift its roots, but instead, its trunk absorbed the obsidian dagger, and the oaken sword darkened. Vahly hoped that was a good sign. She placed the stone in the next hollow, and the tree took in the gift as easily as the stream takes rain. Again, the sword of oak deepened in color, ebony and emerald shadows rising around its edges. The pine sprig went into the third and final hollow, and when the last gift disappeared into the Sacred Oak, the entire world stilled.

No birds sang or wind blew; it was as if the tree held its breath. The cool ground under Vahly's bare feet ceased its drumming, matching the silence inside her.

She trembled, a chill creeping into her like a forgotten ghost. This entire quest and her Blackwater mark too were all a grand fool's game. A bad bet. A wrong card. Dice rolling off the table when she'd gambled it all.

Had she done something wrong? She could imagine that in a moment, the whole circle of holy land would erupt like the volcanoes of old. Fire would rain down. All would be lost.

The oaken sword fell from the tree trunk into her hands.

Her breath caught in her throat as the sword lay across her open palms. The blade, hilt, and pommel—all were made of oak. The grain on the blade wasn't simply lines of growth though. The layers of wood connected here and there, looping and swirling to form a scene. A gaunt woman in a rippling cloak reached a skeletal hand toward a kneeling supplicant. The kneeling figure held a shell. Ah. It was a sea kynd. The gills etched into the neck were so tiny, they were difficult to discern. An undulating line ran from the feet of the standing woman across the face of the sea kynd, below the eyes. So this was a sea kynd female reaching from shallow water to hand a shell to a human. Vahly's brow furrowed.

The image to the right, farther down the oaken blade, showed a hunched and scaled figure—a dragon, surely—walking beside an elf with sharply pointed ears. The elf gestured toward a spot of darker wood. A cave?

A third rendering of the four kynd placed them in a

circle with lines drawn to link each of the kynd to the other, every pair having their own connection that crossed the others.

The carvings were warm to the touch like the creatures shown lived and breathed. A breath shuddered out of Vahly.

Arc's presence announced him before his velvet voice rose. "What does the oaken sword reveal to you, my queen?"

She bit her lip. "The sea can give me food when I need it. The elves can lead dragons to deep caves where earthblood flows. We must all work together to survive."

Arc was nodding when she turned and stood, still holding the sword with open palms.

"It won't be easy," he said. "The land kynd might come together, but we are about to slay scores of sea folk. Aside from General Lilia's handful of rebels, those under the waters will see us only as enemies."

"I'll have to find a way to work with Lilia to get them to cooperate. That is, if we even make it through the last fight."

She gripped the hilt properly, and heat burst across her Blackwater mark. Magic surged up her legs, racing from the earth and into her body. Power blazed down her arms and into her fingers, filling her heart and drumming, drumming, drumming.

The scent of turned earth, new oak leaves, ripe acorns, wet stone, spicy minerals, and the musk of land beasts engulfed her, the sound of the earth's heartbeat rising to a crescendo before settling into a quiet, comforting hum in the back of her mind.

She opened her eyes, and the others were staring at her. Power weighed down each of her fingers like rings of gold and banded her head like a diadem heavy with gems. "My magic is fully awake."

Nix rubbed her hands together. "Now let's see what you can do."

CHAPTER 16

Kicking her webbed toes lightly in the water, Lilia gripped the rock shelf beneath the Sacred Oak's island, her sharp nails digging into the sandy surface. Up there somewhere, a human was gaining more power than any other being. And she prayed to the Source Vahly would remember to uphold the balance and somehow save what could be saved of Lilia's kynd. Her stomach clenched, and she squeezed her eyes shut. It was worth the risk to destroy Astraea. If Astraea lived on and won, there would be no sea folk in that world either. None to care for. None that should be alive. Astraea choked the life from their culture, reaping its pleasures for her own and crushing the spirit of anyone who stood in her way. The sea queen had destroyed all but one human, and that babe who had survived was their only chance at a life as it was meant to be.

The water and the rock shook, and she was jostled

from her perch. Magic echoed from the land, into the salt water, pushing Lilia backward.

Her fellow rebels, likewise shoved through the currents, swam forward, thrusting through the wave of power Vahly must have released when she took hold of the oaken sword the Watcher had foretold.

Yenn's eyebrows knitted, and she dragged her spear through the water, coming abreast of Lilia. "She'll end us all." Her eyes raised, dark gaze on the surface above.

"Even if she does, it would be the same outcome as allowing Astraea to continue on her path of destruction and madness. Astraea will end us certainly. At least we have a chance at balance with Vahly. You were there when the Watcher spoke of her."

Yenn's eyes narrowed. "The Watcher speaks in riddles and with such vagaries that it's impossible to uncover the meaning in her visions."

"Do you want to go back to Astraea? I won't stop you."

"No. No, I don't. I just…"

"I know. I worry too. We'd be fools not to worry. But believe me when I say anyone who went against Grystark and Ryton both must be truly be mad."

Yenn smiled sadly, her gaze on the pinkie coral ring Grystark had given her when she was a child. "They loved our kynd fully."

"Above themselves, and Astraea proved her inability to reign when she murdered them in cold blood."

Yenn swam backward a stroke, eyes wary. "You won't

get reckless on me when the day to face Astraea comes. I don't want to lose you, too. Not if I don't have to."

Lilia's heart warmed, and she touched Yenn's shoulder. "I will be wise." The words felt a little bit like a lie on her tongue. If she had to act rashly to crush Astraea, she would do it. No doubt. But Yenn didn't need to lose sleep over it. Not yet.

"How exactly will the Earth Queen set the balance?" Yenn asked.

"She will need to drive the seawater from her land and raise the old human cities from the ocean. As soon as we talk to her or the Elven King, we will set to work clearing those areas of our kynd so all will be safe."

"How?"

"I have ideas. We'll need to make those areas unlivable."

"With creatures? We could drive lightning fish and sharks into those places."

"Yes, with beasts like that, ones we can herd with magic, and also with spirit warding."

Yenn's mouth opened. "I thought spirit warding was only a story."

"I've done it once. With Grystark."

"For Astraea?"

"Yes. I can do it again. I remember the spell."

"I'm sure it's pretty unforgettable."

Lilia sighed, bubbles leaving her mouth to rise to the surface. She drove upward. "They should come down to speak with us soon."

Yenn swam beside her. "The Elven King is handsome for a land kynd."

Lilia smiled. "He is indeed."

"Since there are no other humans, will the Earth Queen make children with him? Has that ever been done? To create half-elves?"

"Not to my knowledge, but this Earth Queen seems to be rather fond of being the first to accomplish a task."

A grin tugged up one side of Yenn's mouth. "I like that."

"I do too, Yenn. I do too."

CHAPTER 17

Vahly put the tip of the oaken sword against the damp earth. Magic tingled down her fingers where she'd closed them around the warm, smooth hilt, and the power urged her to draw. "I'm having the strangest desire to make pictures in the dirt like a youngling."

Nix put a hand on a hip. "Eh, younglings are more open to magic than grown ones give them credit. Give in to it, Queenie. What's on your mind?"

Vahly began to draw with the sword's sharp, wooden point, sliding it sideways here and there to use the edge of the blade as well. "The Lapis caves, the city of thieves, the ciderhouse. I long to see their roots, if not their walls, whole again. Maybe the earth can welcome our lost, and those dragons can feed the ground and we can see it all grow anew."

Her head swam with the longing, chest aching. This almost felt like a dream or as if she'd had one too many ciders, but with one hand on Kyril, she allowed herself to draw and draw and draw, giving in to the strange urge, the magic coursing through her bones and blood, the love pounding in her heart.

Slowly, the world she'd grown up in materialized in ridges, circles, and lines drawn on the ground. The Lapis palace with its towering doors and labyrinth of corridors were shown in little rivulets of dirt. There were the cliffs that had once overlooked the sea instead of drowning in it. The slim path through the edge of the Red Meadow, near the Fire Marshes, that led to the Dragon's Back and Nix's ciderhouse. The multitude of doors and stairways that snaked along the outside of the city of thieves where the Call Breakers had lived and laughed.

She raised her head to see Arc's mischievous gaze locked onto her, a spark in his eye raising a question. "You know why I'm being led to do this, don't you?"

A dimple appeared beside his grin, and his eyebrows lifted for a moment as he shrugged. "I have an educated guess."

Nix huffed. "Elves. Just tell her, King Arc."

"I don't think that will be necessary," he said.

Amona turned her head like she'd heard something, and then the ground began to tremble. The sacred oak shook off rich brown and deep red leaves that twisted in the wind to surround Vahly. A boulder rose from the dirt like the back of a great turtle, and Aitor gasped, gaze on the horizon.

Everyone turned as the surface of the new sea

shivered and began to spread apart. Foaming waves grew higher and higher, pulling the water from the drowned land and showing the gentle slope of the Red Meadow and the uneven banks of the Silver River.

Vahly held her breath as the water shrank away from the steep incline leading to the Lapis palace.

"The doors. I can see the doors." But of course she couldn't truly see them. It was all much too far away. But she knew where they were, familiar as her fingerprint. She gripped Arc's hand.

Amona strode to the edge of the magically protected island, her chest heaving and her wings rising and falling.

The ground shook hard, and Vahly stumbled, allowing Arc to take her arm.

The Dragon's Back appeared as the seawater receded. Nix held her closed fists to her mouth. From here, they couldn't see what remained of the ciderhouse. It was too far away.

More gray and craggy peaks of the Lapis territory appeared as the ocean pulled back its storm-hued cloak. Vahly's chest clenched; this was too much. To hope that this would last was the most dangerous thing yet...

Shapes moved along the magically dried land.

"What is that?" Nix flew a few feet into the air and squinted as Illumahrah's trees began to grow right before their eyes.

Aitor laughed. "Deer. There are deer coming right up out of the ground! Look near that stand of beech trees.

And there, near the filling pool beside that slope. Is that a ram?"

Vahly's mouth hung open. It was too much to take in, to understand. Rabbits and frogs and snakes and beetles leapt from the formerly drowned earth. Butterflies and falcons soared over trees that were suddenly fully grown. Soon, the newly born Illumahrah would block most of their view of the massive island. The water continued to flow away from the land, then Vahly remembered her sea folk allies.

"Lilia!" She rushed to the edge of the island where the magical seam in the water began. Getting on hands and knees, the sword gripped in her hand and pressing against her fingers, she shouted over the waves and the incredible wind gusting across the retreating water. "Lilia!"

Two heads broke the surface—Lilia's dark hair braided away from her scarred face and another female whose blue hair was shocking in its brightness.

"We are here. What is your plan? What do you wish for us to do?" Lilia held something to her gills, her voice a barely audible croak.

The other female dipped back under the water.

Lilia swam closer, her webbed fingers on the island's wet rocks. "We can lure Astraea for you."

"Only if you're set on surviving. I don't want any outright sacrifices right now."

"We have escaped her so far," Lilia said, her face grave.

Vahly twisted her head to see Amona, Nix, and Arc beside her, their faces pale. "We'll cut Astraea off from the sea's Blackwater well. Ryton told me of it. You go first, Lilia, and fill yourselves with magic, you and your rebels."

Lilia's eyes widened. "You won't destroy it."

"No. I swear it. Now, forced to guess, I'd say Astraea will send three or four units of fifty to deal with you, not knowing we are in the area. She'll want to smash you, to show off a bit, but she won't bother with bringing the whole army of one thousand. When she sees us and fears we will destroy the well, she'll grow reckless."

A wicked smile curved Lilia's lips. "You do know our enemy."

"Only too well. And now I'm equipped to go against her wild power. You lure Astraea there. Be loud about your movement toward the sea's Blackwater well. We will come up behind the warriors she sends after you," she said to Lilia. "When do you think Eux and the rest of our army will arrive?" Vahly asked Amona.

"Once Eux sees this land revealed, she will begin the journey. She will come here with the warriors and anyone else capable of fighting. We will leave word of our movements here on a scroll beneath the oak."

Nix frowned. "Shouldn't we wait to attack Astraea's troops until Eux is here?"

Amona shook her head, her Blackwater mark, so much like Vahly's, shimmering. "No. This will be a surprise. I want to throw Astraea off, to shake her. We'll weaken the army, take out the two hundred or so she brings, then retreat. We'll return here and regroup. I think it's a good strategy, reducing their numbers for the final attack."

"Exactly," Vahly said. "And she won't send her entire force to go after only Lilia and her small band of rebels. We'll annihilate the entirety of the unit Astraea sends."

The furrow between Arc's eyebrows smoothed. "I do think a retreat to this place is a wise move. It feels truly protected. General Lilia, do you have a possible position for retreat as well?"

Lilia sucked a breath, her secondary eyelids spanning across her brilliant irises. "I do. A rift west of the Blackwater. Ryton once showed it to me. Now, I must go. When do we move?" The land was clearing quickly, and the sea pressed the sea kynd female back.

"Now," Vahly said, raising her voice. "I am finished waiting to become her victim."

Amona touched Vahly's back and gave a contented smile, though her gaze spelled death to Astraea.

Vahly stared at Lilia as the waters began to peel away from the island, drawing the rebel sea folk away in the current. "I will leave for the underwater Blackwater well in one day. Be ready. Signal us with a spear to the sky when you see Astraea's warriors approaching."

Lilia's gaze lighted on Amona, then Arc, before returning to Vahly's face. The sea kynd nodded. "Agreed."

Without another rough-sounding word, she disappeared into the retreating sea.

Kyril sat beside Vahly, his eagle eyes darting as he gazed over the recovered land. He sent Vahly an image of them flying, green fire rippling from his mouth and her sword raised above her head.

She set a hand on his neck, then smoothed the soft feathers there. "Yes. It is time to fight, my friend. Time to fight."

CHAPTER 18

Beneath the stars, Arc left the others to their warm fire and dice and found Vahly under the moon-drenched boughs of the Sacred Oak. The elven lands spread beyond the oak, fully restored by her hand. For that alone, he would love her. But his heart said so much more.

"May I?" He gestured toward the spot next to her.

Her bright eyes found his and made his breath catch. "I was hoping you'd show up." She pet Kyril's rump as he stood. "Why don't you keep Nix company for a bit? Nip her if she tries to gamble the rest of the cider away to Aitor."

"I heard that!" Nix's voice carried over the snapping fire and the conversation between Amona and Aitor.

Vahly grinned, watching Kyril lope away. She tugged Arc's cloak, and he let her pull him to the ground rather roughly. She tucked a fallen strand of honey-colored hair behind her round ears. Human ears were odd, but hers were lovely, curved like lilac snail shells. His fingers longed to touch her ear, her proud chin, that graceful neck.

He swallowed and looked at her oaken sword. "Is the magic settled within you?"

Her hand went to her chest, where she ran a thumb over her cloak's hook clasp. "It feels like I've always had it. Like... Maybe it was always there."

"So it truly was sleeping within you."

"I suppose so." Her cheeks pinked, which was unusual for her.

The brief bashfulness warmed him more than he'd ever admit. "Why aren't you gambling with the rest of them? I thought that was your favorite pastime."

They had to wait to join Lilia, so they'd agreed to remain together here, planning to take watches in turn if sleep deigned to welcome them.

Vahly leaned against the oak, lowered her chin, and gazed at him through her thick lashes. "Gambling might not be my favorite pastime anymore."

A unique warmth traveled down his chest, and he raised a knee, feigning nonchalance. "Do tell, my queen. What might hold your attention tonight?"

A grin lengthened her rosy lips. He was incredibly proud that he was the reason for the expression. The longing to press his mouth to hers surged high inside of him.

"Let's forget the world for a moment, Elven King."

"You took the words from my mouth, Earth Queen."

He swept her onto his lap so that their stomachs touched. He set his cheek on her chest and listened to the beat of her powerful heart. She wrapped herself around him tightly.

"I wish we could stay like this forever," he whispered.

He felt her smile against his hair, the magic of his crown spinning and warming his temples. "Me too," she said quietly.

Reaching up, he slipped a hand behind her neck and pulled her mouth to his. Her lips were as sweet as plums and soft, yielding. She tangled her hands in his hair and kissed him firmly.

"I am yours, Arcturus," she promised, turning his heart to gold. "No matter how this ends up. You are stuck with me."

He took her cloak from her shoulders and ran a hand down her back, feeling the trim muscles along her spine through her clothing. He couldn't bear the thought of anyone injuring this dear body. "And I am yours, Vahly. Always."

Shrugging out of his own cloak, he leaned to make sure they were hidden in the darkness, away from the group. Seeing the others fully engaged in what looked like a wild game of dice that had somehow involved breathing fire as well, he settled against the oak and tugged his surcoat tunic off. The cool air found the seams of his linen tunic. Vahly's hands slid over his chest and down his sides, her fingers rumpling the fabric. She kissed his collarbone, sending the scent of turned earth into his nose, then she pressed herself to him. He wanted more, but this was enough. The closeness, the intimacy of the embrace.

Cupping her head in his hands, he stared into her big, searching eyes. "What are you wondering about? I can practically see the questions dancing in your gaze." She tried to look away, but he held her gently. "Don't be ashamed. Ask. I am yours to command."

"What will happen when we...if we have children?"

His own chuckle surprised him. "Then our young will be half-human and half-elf."

"Is that all right? Will they live?"

"I would think so. I don't know that it's been done in the past, but I don't see why not. Our bodies, their chemistry, are not so different."

She gripped his belt and kissed him, taking his breath. "I hope you're right."

"It will be a grand experiment, our mating."

Her laugh echoed off the boughs of the great tree. "Please don't call it that." She looked down at him, her eyes like stars.

He raised an eyebrow, snaked an arm around her waist, and tugged her very, very close. "I find it intriguing."

She opened her mouth to say something else, but with his body issuing orders, he quieted her with another kiss.

CHAPTER 19

A straea grabbed the door of the Watcher's potion cabinet and ripped it free, sending bottles of potion and nets of brightly colored plants into the eddies snaking through the sea cave. The Watcher was missing, and she just knew the crone had gone off to aid the rebels.

"Traitors! All of them!" With a fist, she smashed a sealed shell, scattering obsidian powder and sea herbs into the water around her and General Venu, who remained still, his black hair floating around his stern features. "And what are the fools playing at? They must know the Earth Queen will destroy them if I don't do it first. Idiots!"

Venu swam forward. "What about the balance?" His voice was quiet, as if he were trying to soothe her.

She bared her teeth. "There is no such thing. Not anymore." Turning away, she swam back and forth through the Watcher's sea cave, the dim light of glowing algae clawing to break from the absolute darkness of the corners. "The human is drunk on her power. Isn't it obvious?"

Vines held a coral vase against the wall. She grabbed it, pulled it from its bindings, then slammed it against the scrying bowl in the center of the room. Glaring through the floating remnants at Venu, she stalked toward him. At least the fool held his ground.

"The Earth Queen has already taken back three-fourths of the land," Astraea said. "She'll reclaim the rest as soon as the sun rises, then set her gaze on what else she might control. Mark my words. There will be no end to it! I can't understand why Lilia and her rebels don't see the truth!"

"Perhaps if the Watcher is indeed with them, the crone will enlighten the rebels."

"Lilia has lost what little mind she had. The Watcher could tell her the human will bleed the world dry, and Lilia would twist the information to suit her and her hapless pursuit of revenge. If I had known how she'd mourn those scars we gave her, I'd have simply cut her throat to spare us the trouble."

"You don't think she acts based on her grief over Grystark's death?"

"Lilia doesn't have the depth of mind or soul to hold such a sentiment. What? You disagree?"

"Of course not, my queen."

She snorted and swam out of the foul-smelling cave. One of Venu's scouts rushed past the bed of wide-leaved sea palms and their glowing algae. The male bowed, kicking his feet out behind him in that new way the younger ones had.

Astraea grimaced. "What is it?" she asked as Venu came up beside her.

"Queen," the scout said, "General. The rebels were seen heading toward our Blackwater well."

Her lip curled. "They are in need of strength, are they? Been working spells to help the Earth Queen? Well, perhaps they are readying to attack us. Who spotted them, and how was it accomplished?"

The scout tipped his head, and his brow wrinkled, scales bunching. "I spotted them, my queen. I...saw them. I'm not sure what you want to know."

She hit him with a glare, and he went still. "Were they attempting to hide their approach, going in one by one, using coral or fish or seaweed to hide themselves? Or did they head in brashly, all in one go with no cover?"

"All swam toward the well as a group in the open water."

"Were they silent or speaking?"

"Speaking."

"As I suspected. They think to draw me into the fight. If I believed Lilia was on her own, with only her pathetic band of rebels, I might only send a unit or two after them. Then the Earth Queen could surprise us with her dragon cohorts and take out those one or two units." A laugh bubbled from her lips. "Venu, shall we interrupt their plans?"

"I would love to."

"We will feign a rather large attack, then I'll allow myself to be captured."

"But why?" Venu glanced at the scout.

Astraea looked to the sea's surface. They were so slow of wit sometimes. "The Earth Queen needs my blood, given willingly. She won't kill me, and I will get close to her. Very close. Close enough to take the one weapon that has made her my near equal in power. I will steal the oaken sword."

CHAPTER 20

The sky paled as dawn pushed night away. Vahly and Arc had fallen asleep side by side under the Sacred Oak, and she truly wished the night could last longer. She reached over and lifted a leaf from his hair. One of his eyes cracked open, and his mouth twitched into a half grin that made her heart turn over.

"Trying to wake me, are you?" He put an arm around her and pulled her close.

His scent of mint and summer in the forest blended with the perfume of the earth's magic, which was so strong here. As he ran a finger down the side of her face, her heart beat double time, drawing a grin from him.

She scowled. "You can actually hear my heart speeding up, can't you, elf?"

"Only because I'm so focused on you." He nipped her ear with gentle teeth, and warmth soared down her neck and chest. "I like that I affect you so. It's not as if you don't thrill me, my queen."

He pressed his mouth to hers, and her body melted against him as she reveled in the feel of his power and the knowledge of who he was even without a crown.

She pulled away, then traced his sharp chin with her thumb. Only elves had such sharp features. The beauty of his kynd was nearly painful. "Please don't die today, all right?"

His chest rumbled with a laugh. "I'll do my best."

"You'd better. Or I'll invoke some wonderfully horrible punishment." She untangled herself from his embrace and began strapping her weapons into place. Thankfully, her belt had a loop that fit the oaken sword nicely.

Arc did the same, tucking knives here and there.

Amona and Aitor spoke quietly over a new fire that crackled and sent yellow flames around what appeared to be a deer carcass. Nix slept nearby, sprawled on a stretch of bright green moss.

"And what magic did you work to find that for breakfast?" Vahly asked. The lands had indeed blossomed and sprouted and greened while she slept. She blinked at the expanse of trees that grew right before her eyes. She elbowed Arc, who was fussing with his dagger.

He looked up, then his mouth fell open. "Vahly."

"Yeah."

His grin was so wide it nearly touched the edges of his ethereal crown. "It's coming back. My home."

She smiled, light filling her as if he'd poured his magic into her with his delight.

Amona lifted a hand in greeting. "I hope you don't mind that we hunted on your lands, King Arcturus."

"Of course not," he answered. "I'm amazed at the magic that has brought deer to life here, fully grown. It's a good thing they're here in abundance. I wondered how you would fare with the supplies we had."

Vahly gently kicked Nix's foot. "Rise and fly, Mistress of Cider and Snores."

Nix's yellow eyes flashed open, pupils dilating. Vahly stepped back, grinning as Nix sat up, looking annoyingly gorgeous considering they'd slept rough.

"You're lucky I'm sworn to you, Queenie. Earth Queen or not, it's a dangerous move to wake a sleeping dragon."

"So I've heard, but today will be packed to the rim with dangerous moves. I figured why not toss in one more."

Nix smirked and threw Vahly a waterskin. "Looks like those lips of yours could use some cool water."

Vahly's cheeks heated as she drank a few swallows, determined to ignore Nix's jab.

They tucked into a meal of slightly scorched venison with pockets of hot grease, a few chewy, dried bites of the bacon-flavored plant they'd discovered in the western mountains, and some of Amona's usual morning drink. Vahly had never liked the stuff and really had no idea why her mother loved the burnt bean drink. The hazelnuts—roasted and powdered—she added didn't mask the bitterness. Arc drank his portion and Vahly's too, claiming that with the western plant and bean drink, he was more alert and could see farther than he had in days.

"Can you see my ciderhouse?" The ache in Nix's voice pained Vahly.

Arc looked that way, then faced Nix. "If I'm not mistaken, the foundation remains, and the orchard is sprouting as we speak."

Nix stared at the fire, which snapped like it acknowledged her attention.

Aitor cleared his throat, worried gaze on Nix. "How will we find the sea folk's well?"

Vahly wiped her hands on a clump of fine grass. "I'm hoping we can feel it. And then we should see Lilia's signal from the water when Astraea's warriors arrive."

Aitor stood and clasped his hands in front of him. His long dragon nails had rough ends like they'd broken off—maybe during the evacuation. "Could you raise earthblood for us so we'll be our strongest for this fight?"

She shrugged. "I'll give it a try." Facing the Sacred Oak, she said, "Don't fault me if I rend your island in two."

"You don't really think that's a risk, do you?" Nix's question was obviously for Vahly, but the dragon eyed the tree like it might offer an answer too.

"A risk worth taking."

Vahly unsheathed the oaken sword, walking a ways from the oak and the area they'd chosen for camp. Lavender grew here, nodding new, purple heads as she passed. She imagined the veins of fire snaking through the ground, deep, deep below, then plunged the sword into the earth.

Rumbling like a sudden storm surrounded her, the magic drumming loud in her ears and chest. The lavender spilled to one side, uprooted as steam shot from a fissure. Vahly stepped back quickly, heat rising to singe her cheeks and hands. She retreated to where the rest stood beside the dying fire and watched as a pool of golden earthblood gurgled and announced its presence. Dragon magic—charcoal-scented and sharp like lemon —whirled into the air, and the dragons strode toward the earthblood, eyes glittering.

They gathered around the steaming pool, glancing at one another warily before disrobing and shifting into their full dragon forms. Making a loose circle, they settled comfortably and closed their eyes to allow their specific type of power to flow into them, increasing the strength of the dragonfire banked in their bellies and their physical abilities as well. A dragon fully sated on earthblood was always faster and hardier than one who'd been denied such magical stores. Nix opened her eyes to look around, then lifted her head. Wings lifting slightly, she snuffled in the turned dirt to reveal what appeared to be a large chunk of lapis lazuli.

Well done, Queenie. I feel truly spoiled now. Her dragon lips pulled sideways into a grin.

Amona's head shifted, and she nosed a mounded area of lavender before picking a rough block of jade from the ground. *I will set it by the Sacred Oak for Matriarch Eux as a gift for her upon arrival.*

Once the dragons were ready, the group took off toward the sea with Kyril supporting Vahly and Arc and the dragons in their full forms. They'd left their belongings at the oak, not wanting any distractions during this skirmish.

As they flew, the Forest of Illumahrah grew greener. Leaves burst from the canopy like offerings to the blue sky, and vines dotted with ruby and silver flowers spread along a riverbank.

Soon, they were in sight of the white-capped waters, and it was time to engage their enemy.

CHAPTER 21

Vahly squeezed Kyril's sides with her legs, urging him to leave the land and the resting dragons to circle over the sea again. The underwater Blackwater well pulsed with power beneath the choppy waves, tugging at the mark on her forehead. But so far, there had been no signal from Lilia that Astraea had been seen. They had to stay out of sight as best as possible to retain the element of surprise.

"You're watching out for the spear, right?" she twisted to ask Arc. "Those elven eyes will catch it, I'm sure." One of Lilia's rebels would propel their spear out of the sea and into the air when they spotted the enemy.

His gaze on the distant waters, Arc ran his fingers up Vahly's side and down again in a movement that seemed unconsciously done on his part. "I am," he said. "I don't know whether to hope the sun sets before they arrive. I could use light magic in the water to blind the sea kynd, but, of course, it would likewise render Lilia and her rebels temporarily sightless."

"Oh, because their eyes are so sensitive to light," she said. "I remember the feeling."

Arc's hand tightened on her waist, and he pressed a quick kiss to the back of her neck. "I should've thought to mention that in our meeting with the rebels."

"We can use it at some point, I'm sure. It's a good plan."

Kyril turned to fly back to the rocky coastline, which was a sheer drop nearly as black as the obsidian cathedral in the drowned city of Bihotzetik. A thought slid through Vahly's mind. She would like to bring Bihotzetik from its watery grave, to revive it and fill it with life, to possibly even create a spire of her own on the cathedral near the other Earth Queen's spires.

The signal! Flying just above the shoreline, Amona shouted in Vahly's head.

Vahly spun Kyril around and unsheathed the oaken sword as the rebel spear began its return descent into the waves, called back by the spell of its owner.

The ocean rumbled, and chills swept over Vahly as the dragons joined her in the darkening sky. "Watch for Lilia. Be careful not to harm her warriors!"

A line of three rebels leapt from the water to dive under again, bright red spears pointed and the sea hissing around them in some magical attack on Astraea's incoming force. The ocean shivered as hundreds of dark shapes swam just below the surface toward the Blackwater well.

This was far more than one unit sent to deal with a small band of rebels. The Sea Queen had brought what looked like a thousand warriors. A triangular shadow slid under the curling waves, as large as Kyril. A tail whipped behind it, breaking the water with a barbed tip. Beside the sea monster, over a dozen sharks cut the dark blue currents with shimmering fins and incredibly quick, lithe movements.

Vahly's stomach turned, and her palm sweat as she held on to the oaken sword. "Now! Attack the rear guard!"

Kyril and the dragons speared the citrine and smoke sky, soaring high over the back of the sea army. One by one, the dragons dropped low to blow dragonfire into the waves. Lightning crackled above, throwing silver like coins over the bloody water. Spears rose from twisting columns of liquid to send spelled salt water at them. Nix narrowly dodged a hand of magicked water, then locked eyes with Vahly.

Vahly pointed the sword at the charcoal cliffs, and the rock bent and rose from the earth, spreading wings that echoed the shape of Kyril's. With a stone beak, her creation shrieked and took off into the sky. Arc spun three spheres of air magic, then threw them at the stone gryphon and into the space in front of Kyril. At once, Nix blew fire, Kyril roared, and the stone gryphon opened its beak over the rows of swimming sea kynd under his black belly. Amethyst and sage fire rippled from the stone beast's maw and blasted into the ocean. Over the sound of thunder and shrieking, Vahly heard a voice.

"Come for me, Earth Queen!" Astraea raised herself on a shimmering wave, spear outstretched, the water glistening over her face like a thin veil. Her blood-red lips parted as she rose higher and higher, ignoring their attack on her army. "Come for me!"

The urge to spin and direct everything at Astraea pulsed in Vahly's blood, but what Kyril did, the stone gryphon mimicked. She had to continue fighting at the rear line, to stick to their strategy. If not, this full force would hit Lilia and her rebels.

Vahly's team unleashed another blast of dragonfire and green fire, and the water bubbled and steamed, bodies of sea folk turning to ash or floating half scorched. The sharks turned on their masters, teeth glinting in the sunset light and tails thrashing.

Pointing the oaken sword at the sea, Vahly commanded the earth to rise. The magic lunged inside her heart like she held a dragon in between her ribs. Waves parted as a mound of the seabed broke the currents and spilled earthblood across the battlefield. The water hissed as the earthblood touched it, and the giant, arrow-headed sea monster veered away from the glowing, golden heat, one slimy fin rising high and nearly catching Astraea as it turned.

A unit of Astraea's warriors blasted spelled salt water toward Aitor and Amona. Kyril shrieked and tipped suddenly, Vahly and Arc having to grip tightly to his pelt to keep their seats. The stone gryphon's movements loosely followed Kyril's, and the great beast of earth magic tipped its impossible wings. Feathers of granite and dark crystal blocked the flow of deadly salt water, pushing the magicked wave back, where it crashed on those who'd spelled it. Bodies were pitched across the surface, limbs snapping at odd angles and screams going silent.

Lilia appeared briefly at the surface as the rebels pushed a crescent-shaped wave—obviously brought forth with spells—toward Astraea's warriors. The water in front of the Sea Queen's uneven line of fighters bubbled violently in response, and the wave surged back toward Lilia's group. Astraea's plume of seawater, the column that carried her, rushed toward Vahly, Arc, and Kyril. Vahly pointed the oaken sword, and rock from the depths sheared the glassy swells to surround Astraea in a cage of stone pillars.

They had the Sea Queen, caged, trapped.

CHAPTER 22

Kyril roared, and the stone gryphon echoed the ear-splitting sound as it veered westward.

Vahly held her breath, waiting for Astraea to defend herself, to call up the sea and swallow everyone whole. What could Vahly do if the Sea Queen did this? Could the sword raise enough land to thwart such a move?

The sea quieted. The creatures swam away. The warriors on both sides stilled beneath the stone cage.

A layer of salt water undulated over Astraea's body and face. Her eyes had gone flat black, and her red lips tightened into a straight line as she stared at Vahly.

Swallowing, Vahly urged Kyril closer. This was probably a trap. It had been too easy to capture the Sea Queen. The stone gryphon flew above them, a shadow of protection darkening the glistening water and the glow of the sun's last rays on the pillars of Astraea's prison.

Vahly's magic surged inside her, and she saw a flash,

a vision. Webbed fingers. A sea kynd slicing its own palm. Blood flowing onto the oaken sword.

"I can see you believe you've won, human." Astraea's voice was harsh as it crossed her thin, magical barrier of water to carry on the wind. "But I must submit to the balance by freely offering my blood to your fine weapon there. And that, I will never do."

Run her through, Queenie! Nix soared above the cage, eyes catching the sunset's last gasp. *To hell with the balance!*

Believe me, Nix, I want to. But I can't rush into this. Not after what Lilia told Arc. There is no other Blackwater-marked sea kynd to take her place and share her blood with the sword. My magic tells me the ritual must happen. My stomach turns inside out when I consider any other alternative.

Vahly bumped Kyril with a heel, sending him in a gentle dive toward the rebels. Lilia's head appeared above the surface. The rebel leader placed two leaves on her gills and watched Vahly expectantly.

"Have you heard anything new from your Watcher?" Vahly asked. "Any news on a newly born Sea Queen?"

Lilia shook her head. "The Watcher is hidden far from here. We've had no word or update. I hate the fact, but Astraea must be kept alive until we can persuade her to give up a portion of her blood. Only then will all kynd live in harmony."

Vahly gritted her teeth. "She won't do it. How are we supposed to talk her into this?"

The rebel leader set a cold gaze on Vahly. "This is war. Use what she loves to bend and break her."

"What does that beast of a female love?"

"Her singer, Larisa."

Kyril flew up and over the rebels, then floated on an air current back toward Lilia.

"A singer?"

Lilia dipped beneath the water, then rose again. "Astraea loves her like a prized possession. If you threaten the singer, then perhaps Astraea will yield."

But they had to get their hands on this singer first. Vahly nudged Kyril, and they flew over the enemy army with Astraea at their back. "I will run your queen through if you don't deliver Larisa the singer to me at the coastline by sunrise."

To prove her point, she rushed the cage, oaken sword outstretched.

The sea surged above the enemy army, and shouts rose from the waves.

"I will secure the singer!" a sea kynd female raised her spear. "We will make peace!"

Arc made a noise, and Vahly turned to see his gaze on the one who'd spoken. "So some do long for peace like Lilia and her rebels."

Vahly had Kyril fly around the cage. "Your folk wish for peace. It is your choice whether they receive it. Either way, you have lost. If you won't give your blood, I will simply kill you and suffer whatever consequences the Source may have in store. I won't be fooled into freeing you without that blood." Vahly locked gazes with Amona. "Please set up a watch on her. If you believe we can spare one soul at a time to rest on land, that would be good. We have a long night ahead of us."

Will your stone gryphon remain in the sky? Amona flew beside the massive rock beast, her distance showing her respect for the magical creature's deadly capabilities.

Magic sizzled under Vahly's ribs. *Yes. It will remain where I order it.*

Amona dipped her head, and Vahly was almost certain a proud grin lifted the edge of Amona's snout. *I will do as you order, Earth Queen.*

Nix zipped by and gave a wink.

Vahly mentally ordered the stone gryphon to keep watch, then she turned Kyril toward the coastline, for once feeling like she belonged seated on a rare creature alongside an elven king. *Blooded for the battle,* her birth mother had said of her name so long ago when Amona had rescued her. Her blood did indeed feel crafted for this fight. Power tingled in her fingertips as she sheathed the oaken sword and set her mind to the next fight.

CHAPTER 23

Astraea gripped the stone pillars that held her captive, her blood churning, boiling. How dare the Earth Queen? She shook with the longing to raise every drop of water in the sea and bring it crashing down on Illumahrah where the human was currently plotting with her elf. But the cage did more than trap her physically. Born of earth magic, it pressed on her sea power, smashing her abilities into that of a youngling's. She couldn't have called up a single wave to help herself. She could barely keep the thin layer of water over herself to breathe. And now the human had called on her warriors to fetch Larisa. Would Vahly torture Larisa in an effort to make Astraea comply?

Astraea snorted, then smoothed her hair and readjusted her coral crown. As if she would give up all for one singer. True, it would be a tragedy to lose such a gem as Larisa. And seeing her suffer would prick at Astraea's heart, considering what the female had been through. But to consider allowing the Earth Queen to win?

Never. She'd see Larisa ripped limb from limb before she relented and gave up any blood.

A hiss of spelled water turned Astraea's head. Venu's face appeared at the base of her stone cage, moonlight sliding through the layer of water he held over him and giving him a ghostly look.

"My queen."

"Venu." She kept an eye on the circling dragons. Amona and that horrid stone gryphon were on watch. "They'll see you. You should go. I don't want my warriors without their best general. Go. Now."

"As you wish, my queen, but I beg to hear your strategy now that all this has come to pass."

"I will feign a capitulation when they bring Larisa. Once the human believes I am about to give up my blood and slice my palm, I will rip the sword from her weak hands and escape to the sea."

Venu's lips parted. He glanced at the starry sky where the stone gryphon's massive shadow blocked the moon. "But won't they have you on some sort of land if they plan to force you into submission? Surely, the Earth Queen isn't so foolish as to attempt her move underwater."

"They want this balance more than anything. I will simply request that they allow me to keep this wave, maybe one a touch more comfortable, around me during the ceremony. It is a small request. I doubt they'll argue it when they believe themselves so close to their goal. I will be quite convincing when it comes to my reaction to their torture of Larisa."

"I worry none will believe it, my queen. You're no weakling."

"The land kynd don't see soft emotion as weakness. They are fools, Venu. I tell you. Complete fools. My army won't believe my grief, but the Earth Queen will swallow my poison in full. Tell them to watch and to keep their disbelief to themselves. If they—"

The Lapis matriarch, that disgusting beast Amona, flashed through the sky, low, nearly striking Venu from his wave. Dragonfire blasted over his head, and the heat seared Astraea's cheeks and hands. Venu dove backward in an elegant arc toward the sea far below.

"Curse you, vile lizard!" Astraea lunged back, hating the limit on her magic that kept her from bringing more water to protect herself from the dragonfire.

Shaking, she pulled a breath from the waters through her singed gills. Her hair remained intact and her crown too. She wouldn't be so easily injured. She would survive this, and the dragons, elves, and that Earth Queen would rue the day they tangled with the Sea Queen.

CHAPTER 24

On the shoreline, above the dark cliffs touched by a bleeding sunrise, a cold, salty wind chapped Vahly's face. She stepped closer to Kyril and Arc as she pointed the oaken sword at the stone cage that held Astraea. The rocks groaned and growled as they reshaped themselves over and over again, bringing the cage across the stretch of sea between Sugarrabota and the wide ocean. Gripping the sword with a sweaty hand, Vahly walked toward the stone cage that now sat at the edge of the cliffs. Astraea kept that film of water over her, most likely to continue breathing and to be able to speak more easily.

"Are they bringing Larisa here now? Where is she?" Vahly demanded.

Astraea's eyes blinked slowly, and her gaze traveled the length of Vahly's body like she was searching for weaknesses. Vahly raised her chin and did her best to pretend she wasn't nervous.

Before the Sea Queen could respond, a voice echoed from the crashing waves below. Nix flew high and peered down.

It's the female singer. They've brought her, Nix said.

Vahly joined Nix, walking in the shadow she cast through the morning sun. Vahly raised the sword and brought the singer, Larisa, from the water inside a cupped hand of rock. Water spilled between the stone fingers, only a small portion of liquid remaining to coat Larisa. Amona kept back, flying high because the spelled salt water was still the biggest risk in the dragons' interactions with the sea folk.

With both Larisa and Astraea in front of Vahly and the others, the dark game of strategy began.

Vahly locked eyes with Larisa. The female was slender with large, lovely green eyes and more pronounced fins on her fingers and arms than Astraea or Ryton had. She was pretty but definitely more...fishy. "I don't want to hurt you, but I will if Queen Astraea refuses to give us her blood."

Larisa's gaze flew to Astraea. "Give me your orders, my queen." Her young voice was mellow and songlike even in regular speech, even in the strange sounds of the sea folk's version of the dragon language.

The Sea Queen kept her focus on Vahly, which Vahly found disturbing. "Withstand whatever they decide to do," Astraea said, showing no emotion at all. "Don't be weak. You are of my court, and I will not see you cower."

All Vahly had seen of Astraea was her wild, mad side.

She didn't like this version of the Sea Queen with her quiet voice and cold, calculating looks. Perhaps this whole idea had been a huge mistake, but she had to see it through because there weren't any secondary plans here.

Vahly approached the hand of stone that held the singer. Ignoring the film of spelled salt water that could kill a dragon, she grabbed hold of the singer's hair and forced her to her knees, pointing the oaken sword at the female's throat.

"A touch from this land-blessed weapon will most likely do bad things to your sea-born flesh. You sure you want to lose her singing voice, Astraea?"

Vahly braced herself, stomach churning, then placed the tip of the oaken sword not on the singer's throat, but on her shoulder. Larisa shrieked, eyes squeezing shut.

Stepping back, Vahly held the sword's hilt with both hands to hide her shaking. This didn't feel noble or right. This was something Astraea would do. Vahly had to keep pushing Astraea, she knew that, but how could she when her stomach was about to empty itself all over her own feet?

An uneven circle of purple grew where the sword had touched Larisa, like the weapon had bruised her deeply. The dark color spread throughout her shoulder. If only a touch of the sword did so much, what would a true strike do? Larisa shivered, and Vahly hated herself despite knowing this was all necessary.

I can't do this, she said telepathically to Arc.

Then don't. We'll find another way. Chin tipped down, he watched her with sincere, dark eyes. *Or give me the task, my queen. I would take this horror from you and bear it. It is the least I can do considering how much you've accomplished for me and for the last of my kynd.*

"This won't work, human," Astraea said. "I don't care what you do to her. Yes, it is a shame, a waste. But if you want to hurt me. Hurt *me*." A flicker of knowing danced through the Sea Queen's eyes.

Ryton had died to end this creature. Astraea was responsible for the deaths of over a thousand dragons. Younglings. The innocent. Heat roared into Vahly's blood, and she speared the sword through Astraea's cage, the point a breath from the Sea Queen's cheek. What if Vahly accidentally killed her?

It had to be risked. If not, they'd be in a stalemate.

Steeling herself, Vahly raised her free hand, splayed her fingers, then moved her hand down, feeling the stone cage responding to her, the rock a cool spot in the magic in her chest.

Astraea eyed the ceiling of the cage as it began to drop. "You think to crush me? Fine. If I die, you have no blood to put upon your sword. My generals and warriors will rise up in my place, and there will never be peace."

"I won't kill you. I'm not a fool. Well, not always." She gave Astraea a wink like she used to do with those she'd bet against at the ciderhouse. "Hopefully, I can control myself enough to keep you alive until you decide to capitulate."

"Never." The cage lowered itself onto Astraea's back, and the Sea Queen went to her hands and knees, water splashing around the fins on her lean arms and her fingers as they reached toward her coral spear. Vahly had thrown the weapon beyond the cage.

"You sure about that?" Vahly pressed her hand lower, and the cage groaned, speeding up its descent. Astraea was pinned between the cage's former ceiling and the floor, limbs askew, spear dropped to the ground.

"You'll kill me, idiot human," Astraea squawked.

Vahly gave the stone another small, magical push and heard Nix snort in dark amusement behind her.

The Sea Queen's coral crown snapped in two and fell from her protective layer of water. The scarlet pieces littered the grassy ground around Vahly's boots. Astraea was hissing in her own tongue.

"Ready to shed your blood for peace, Sea Queen?" Vahly knelt beside her. A part of her was enjoying this humbling of a murderer, but another part of her hated it as much as she'd hated injuring Larisa. "Or do you need further persuasion?"

Nix and Arc stepped closer, but Vahly held out a hand.

"Stay back." She wasn't sure what Astraea could still do to hurt them in this position.

Astraea snarled like a wolf. "I'll never relent. Never."

"Please!" Larisa called out. The bruising on her shoulder had already started to fade. "Stop. I beg you. Take my blood."

"Shut your lips, singer!" Astraea rasped, her cheek pressed to the floor and her eyes bulging.

"Your blood would not balance the magic, Larisa," Arc said calmly. "But your willingness to work toward peace is noted."

Larisa whimpered, then bit her lip, gaze darting to Astraea.

Vahly pointed the oaken sword at Astraea's fingers. "I wonder if I can drive this spelled water away from you."

"If you do, then I'll suffocate."

"I'm feeling risky."

She willed the water away from the land, calling up the land's energy to block the flow of sea magic. Power like sparks of fire heated her Blackwater mark between her eyebrows and tingled across her fingertips. The water peeled away from Astraea's hand like a shed glove. Vahly pushed the energy farther up Astraea's exposed form until one arm was bare to what Ryton had called the raw air, as well as the Sea Queen's gills, lips, and nose. Astraea gasped, mouth opening and closing, gills spread wide on the one side of her neck that was visible.

Then the Sea Queen went still, eyes wide.

Amona flew in a low circle above them. *Could she be acting as though the injury is worse than it is?*

"That's what I'm worried about," Vahly said.

"Quick, Queenie! Let that magic go." Nix came forward.

"Get back," Vahly scooted closer and tried to reverse what she'd done. It was far easier to accomplish earth magic on a grand scale rather than doing these small tasks. She attempted to coax the land's energy into resting again, but it wasn't working.

Astraea thrashed weakly, her eyes rolling up. Vahly focused on her earth magic, but the water wouldn't return. Going limp, Astraea gasped once. Then the Sea Queen went completely still.

Astraea was dead.

Vahly stared at the Sea Queen's gray face. A bead of sweat rolled down Vahly's back, and she flicked the sword to break the stone cage apart. Nix was suddenly at her side. Vahly turned to urge her backward, still reeling, afraid, and then water was coursing from the cliffs across the grass. A tendril of seawater shot toward Nix. Vahly lunged to block it with her body. The spelled water ripped the oaken sword from Vahly's hand.

CHAPTER 25

L ilia gritted her teeth as she fought Astraea's warriors. There were so many of them. But victory was in sight. The Earth Queen had captured Astraea. Finally, the Sea Queen would be humbled, then she would be killed, and the sea would be a far better place because of it. Spear outstretched and the scent of blood and dragonfire in her gills, Lilia spun in the water and spat one last spell. Her magicked current whirled around five large males, twisting their bodies in a powerful eddy and tearing their spears from their hands. The rebels in a half circle around her cheered and let out their own spellwork so the water bubbled and rushed toward the warriors beside those Lilia had disarmed.

Torn between triumph and agony over attacking her own kynd, she swam hard for the rift, Yenn and the others behind her. It was time for the rebels to retreat. Astraea had brought the entirety of her forces, and with the Earth Queen busy on shore, Lilia and her crew were in a dangerous position. There was absolutely no way they could fight the whole of the sea's army. No, retreat was the best option for now. Hopefully, Queen Vahly would send word on the next step toward peace and the end of the war soon.

A thick band of luminescent seaweed shielded the first appearance of the rift from view. Lilia remembered when Grystark and Ryton had brought her here many years ago. She could almost see them again, laughing with one another, pushing and shoving like brothers. They'd been so young then, their beards only shadows and their bodies showing only a handful of scars. Lilia pushed through the seaweed, startling an ivory eel that hissed and swam quickly past. Yenn made a sound of surprise behind her, and the sizzle of magic told Lilia that Yenn had buzzed the eel to persuade it to move on.

The rift eyed Lilia from the gloom. She swam into the slender, blue-black stretch of water between the towering faces of dark rock, heading into the depths toward the spot where she and Yenn had stored food and extra weapons.

"Astraea is conquered!" Yenn shouted as they all came together in the small alcove shielded by the rift.

Gracus and the others joined in the joyful cries, grabbing one another to shake forearms and boast about this attack or that.

But they were celebrating far too soon. More than anything, Lilia longed to see Astraea dead and floating, but the Sea Queen had fought her way out of tight spots before, and she could manage it again, no doubt.

"As far as we know," Lilia explained, "Astraea hasn't given her blood to the oaken sword. She will fight on, knowing Vahly can't slay her outright. Not now anyway. We shouldn't be patting ourselves on the back quite yet."

The rebels quieted and nodded. Yenn set her spear by a net full of harvested scallops. "What should we be doing?"

"Persuading more of our kynd to join us and the Earth Queen."

Gracus helped himself to a crock of jellied seagrass. The sharp scent of pepper squid ink floated through the water. "How can we figure out who might be willing and communicate with them?"

"We need to infiltrate the ranks of the lowest rung of the army. Those who haven't been shaped by Astraea for quite as long. Those who remember their families and are possibly shocked at how the queen has behaved."

Yenn ate a scallop, then wiped her mouth with the back of her hand. "But our faces are known now."

Lilia swam to the edge of the alcove to check for any pursuit. The water was dark and still. "Then perhaps we can simply put up notices in cities and towns while everyone sleeps."

Standing, Gracus set his seagrass aside and grabbed a length of wide seaweed to bind a cut that appeared to have opened on his forearm. "Yes. We'll ask them to rise up against Astraea and those loyal to her when the Earth

Queen next acts. To show their devotion to our kynd by rejecting war for war's sake and choosing peace."

Pointing a finger, Yenn grinned. "I like that. They get to choose how to support the rebellion. It puts it in their hands, and they can aid us in ways that haven't occurred to us."

Rummaging through the supplies, Lilia found a shell-crate filled with bottles of squid ink. "Everyone knows the spell work for posting notices, yes?" It would be far faster than painstakingly carving messages into the city and town boards. Besides, notices were sanded down on every seventh day. With magic and ink, they could repost the message again easily no matter what schedule the town was on for posting. She doled out the ink and helped the one rebel who couldn't recall the phrasing for the spell as they discussed who would go to which city and town, Gracus taking the places farthest away from the rift, Yenn and Lilia staying close to the rift.

"Go and return quickly," Lilia said. "We can't be gone for long. I must be here if the Earth Queen or King Arcturus needs me."

When they were certain they hadn't been followed and night had come in full, they set out to raise a true rebellion born of ink and courage.

CHAPTER 26

Vahly's heart screamed as she lurched forward to try to grab the sword.

Enclosed in a five-foot wave and suddenly recovered, Astraea cackled as her coral spear flew into her hand. The water—holding the sword, the Sea Queen, and the coral spear—flowed backward, then dove over the cliffs. She was gone and with her, any chance of restoring the balance.

Arc was spinning air magic already, and he appeared to fly after her. Kyril lunged, then soared out of sight in pursuit behind the dragons.

No. That hadn't just happened. It couldn't have. She'd been given the key to saving all the good kynd in the world, and she'd been outwitted and let it slip from her hands. Without a fight. Without a word. Vahly had lost the oaken sword. Astraea had the weapon now, and she was in the ocean, which meant she'd do her best to destroy the sword if the job could be done.

Reaching the edge, gasping as she skidded to a stop, Vahly watched as Arc struggled against the spray of water rising where Astraea must have plunged back into the sea. The dragons didn't breathe fire, Nix and Amona shouting into Vahly's head about fearing to scorch the oaken sword. Arc dropped to the rocks, his distant form shuddering beside the foamy claws of the ocean. Kyril plunged into the water, going after Astraea, and the sight of his disappearing tail dropped Vahly to her knees.

Nix! Please!

Nix flew directly at Vahly, who jumped onto her back, narrowly avoiding the crystalline spines along the dragon's neck and back.

Vahly pulled her dagger from her baldric and commanded the earth to follow Astraea and raise her up. The scent of the sleeping ground under the sea tickled her nose. A sandy mound with bits of blue coral and a floundering black fish appeared through the raucous surface, but Astraea was nowhere to be seen.

"Kyril!" Where was he? What was he thinking?

Nix swooped low where the sea kynd on both sides were beginning to fight again, raising swells of spelled salt water and shooting spears through the air. *I don't see him. What should I do, Vahl?*

Vahly was going to be sick. *Return to shore. We can't get hit right now. I can't think. I don't know what to do.*

They veered west to see Aitor grabbing Arc gently in his talons. Soon, Aitor was flying to the cliffs to meet Vahly and Nix.

But Kyril...

Clenching her stomach with a hand, Vahly leaned over Nix's head, tears threatening to blind her.

Amona roared and blasted Astraea's warriors with a massive band of fiercely orange dragonfire that peeled back the water in great plumes of steam. Shrieks and cries rose.

Kyril burst from the parted water and the steam, soaking wet and struggling to fly. He was alive! Vahly's magic pulled taut, and she willed strength to him, not at all sure if the power worked that way or not. The gryphon shook his wings midair and trailed her as they returned to the coastline, soaring over the sight of Larisa breaking through her stone hand barrier and leaping over the cliffs to the water.

Vahly, Kyril, Arc, and the dragons tumbled to a rest at the Sacred Oak in either one moment or an eternity. It was impossible to know how much time had passed. Vahly rushed to Arc as the sound of wings and shouts filled the late day sky.

Eux, the Jades, the Lapis, and the elves riding atop three Call Breakers landed in the high grass, tucking wings and transforming quickly.

In human form, Eux threw open a bag and quickly donned a loose shirt and wide trousers before hurrying over and giving Vahly a quick bow.

Vahly barely glanced up. Arc's eyes were opening, but he looked gray around the mouth, and his hand was oddly withered. "Tell me what is going on with you. Right now. No more being the tough one, elf. Spill it."

CHAPTER 27

A
rc set his jaw as pain whipped through him. The intensity of this illness, or whatever it was, had made his drop to the cliff's rocky base a mere afterthought. "I don't know. My...difficulties started before we left the northern mountains." He struggled to sit, but then fell back again, panting. A fresh cut along the side of his face had already healed over to a silver scar. That too would be gone soon enough. Sadly, he didn't think this greater problem could be healed. "I should've told you," he said to Vahly, hating the way her lovely eyes pinched as she worried for him and for what they could possibly do to retrieve the oaken sword. "I should've asked my kynd." He fisted his hands, frustrated that he brought yet another problem to the table.

"What happened out there, on the sea?" Eux demanded, eyeing Arc, then Amona and Nix too. They'd transformed and approached now, brows furrowed and faces pale.

Vahly rested a warm hand on Arc's smooth forehead. "The Sea Queen took the sword the Sacred Oak gave me," she answered Eux.

Gasps sounded all around as the land kynd grouped into a rough circle, the Sacred Oak beyond waving in the wind, whispering something like a warning.

Arc cocked an eyebrow at the tree. "A bit late for that. Now, what can we do to get the sword back? Do you have a plan?"

"Of course I don't have a plan. It just happened!" She closed her eyes and took a breath as he slid his good hand over hers. "I don't know," she said. "But with all these brains here, surely we can come up with a strategy to retrieve the sword and to find out how to help you heal whatever this is."

Questions flew at Vahly like arrows, and she answered them all with quick information as best she could. She was so much stronger than she knew. Once silence reigned, Arc raised a finger and looked to Rigel, Haldus, and Ursae.

"Perhaps you could examine me, Rigel? The rest of you, please go about the planning. I beg you not to waste time on me."

Vahly smacked his arm gently, then patted it, grimacing in apology. "You are never a waste of time, fool. You are one of our greatest warriors. We need you."

Rigel studied his withered hand, the older elf's steel-colored hair reflecting the sunlight. "I don't know, my queen, my king. I wish I did. Haldus, will you take a look?"

The shorter elf came forward, then knelt, brown eyes sliding over Arc's face like he might find the answers there. "I have seen this once. In the green years."

A time of rebellion. But it was so long ago…

"What are the green years?" Vahly's throat bobbed as she looked at Arc, so he attempted to smooth his features.

"I was only a boy," Haldus whispered.

Rigel glanced up, eyes wide. "But you're…"

"Old? Yes." Haldus laughed grimly, a rumble deep in his barrel chest.

"I'm wondering what Queen Vahl is. What are the green years?" Nix asked as she tied up the sleeve of a split-legged dress that was wrinkled from being in her bag under the oak.

Haldus sat back on his heels, looking with eyebrows lifted at Vahly. She gave him a nod to continue. She appeared barely able to sit and not run screaming madly. "Back then, two princes warred for the elven crown. They were born twins. The eldest, Eldil, was chosen and crowned, his brother, Tam, swearing allegiance. But when a powerful family supported Tam's claim to the throne, he rebelled against Eldil. When Eldil died during a skirmish, Tam was crowned. In less than two seasons, Tam was dead. It began with a weakness in the hand he raised against his brother the king, then he started to collapse now and again. One night, he went off to hunt with his supporters, and though many suspected he was killed, I saw his body when I worked with the Council's assistants. He had withered away like the life had been sucked from his body by some unseen beast."

Cold speared Arc's chest. "A curse set into the crown?" He blinked and watched Vahly. "It makes sense."

"How?" she asked him. "You had Cassiopeia's blessing when you swore allegiance to me."

He lifted an eyebrow and pressed the pain to the back of his mind. Sitting up, he cleared his throat. "I battled Mattin, an elf to whom I swore allegiance." He brushed a thumb over Vahly's battle-hardened knuckles. Even though she had scars and callouses, she still had the softest skin. He looked up. "Haldus, is there a way I can avoid death?"

Haldus swallowed. "Give up the crown."

If he gave up the crown to Rigel or Haldus, they'd suffer the same fate. If the crown would accept them, that is. They had no royal blood. "Ursae is the only one of us who didn't openly defy Mattin."

Ursae's eyes went wide. She wasn't trustworthy. But she might be his only hope.

Arc stood with Haldus's help. "Ursae, you never denied Cassiopeia's commands, did you?"

The female knelt. "No, my king. I had come to my senses by then."

Rigel's head jerked so he was facing her. "You weren't

robbed of your senses when you first chose Mattin. You knew full well what you were about."

Ursae kept her gaze down. "Yes. Yes, of course. But I didn't fight Cassiopeia."

"Do you have royal blood?" Arc asked.

"I don't know. We were servants to the court. I...I don't think so."

"Then it can't be you. The crown won't accept it, unfortunately for all of us." Arc paced slowly, his legs not quite functioning properly. "Let's put this worry away for now, all. We must focus on how to retrieve the oaken sword. Queen, tell us your thoughts."

Vahly straightened and looked from him to the crowd. "I have learned that through experiment sometimes we can find solutions never before imagined. King Arcturus and Mistress Nix helped me discover how Kyril and the creations we raise from the earth can breathe green fire, a fire similar in strength to dragonfire with properties we haven't fully tested yet."

She walked back and forth in front of her subjects, every inch the muddied, bloodied warrior queen. Arc's heart swelled.

"When I was under the waters," she said. "I watched General Ryton, my captor turned savior, use a certain spell to call back his spear. I'm sure most of us have witnessed the sea folk working this magic during battle, calling their weapons home so they can strike again and again." Her throat moved in a swallow, and Arc guessed she recalled past battles where that particular spellwork had meant death for her beloved Lapis dragons. "Ryton used a three-word spell to temporarily transform me into a sea kynd. As one of them, I was able to mimic some of their spellwork. Perhaps I can find General Lilia of the rebel sea folk and have her work the same spell on me. Then I would maybe have the capability to call the oaken sword as they call their coral spears."

Arc froze. "No. Please."

A few heads turned toward him, and he realized he'd spoken aloud.

"You nearly died there," he said, not feeling kingly, only desperate to never see her in the state she'd been in that prison cell in the sea, the way her eyes had been nearly swollen shut, the blood on her mouth... "It was... Please, let's consider other possibilities."

A sad smile graced her rose petal lips. "I'm open to listening to other ideas, but I won't consider a group going into the sea with me. We can't risk the strategic minds here. You must lead our army. Every last one of you will be needed in the coming days. Even more so if I fail."

But no one spoke up, Amona looking to him, then to Eux, who shook her head.

"I appreciate your courage, Earth Queen." Eux touched a ring holding a two-inch dragon tooth near her jawline. "I can't think of another plan. We cannot be precious about ourselves. This is not only a war. This is the war. We either win or we die."

Arc pressed a hand against his heart, then raised his

head to meet Vahly's intense stare. "Agreed," he said, but he couldn't quite keep the defeat from his voice.

Watching her go back into the sea would be a far worse agony than this curse.

CHAPTER 28

Vahly gripped Kyril's ruff and breathed deeply as he sent her images of them soaring over the renewed Forest of Illumahrah. She patted his side and smiled. "If we live through this, we'll fly every day, my friend. Every single day." The gryphon keened as if begging for her to hurry it up and win the day. "I'm trying, love. I am trying."

She wore only her shirt and trousers. Her boots would only be ruined in the sea, and once she was changed, if this plan worked, she would have fins that didn't allow for her usual vest, socks, and shoes.

Arc was on Nix's back, and Amona flew above them, watching the sea for a possible attack. The wind whipped Arc's black hair, and the moon made his crown blink silver now and then. He appeared fine at the moment, thank the Source. Maybe he was strong enough to fight the curse and live despite what Haldus had said about the ancient elf Tam.

"The rift is just there, if I remember correctly." Arc pointed to a spot that looked no different from the rest of this part of the ocean.

"Elves. Such showoffs," she muttered, trying to act normal for Kyril even though her heart beat frantically. The oaken sword might already be in pieces. They might already be as good as dead, the land swallowed again by Astraea's hand, and all the dragons, elves, and animals drowned.

Kyril shook gently, like he wanted her to stop pretending and joking, as if he knew the truth and didn't want her to treat him like a youngling. She hugged his neck, tucking into his musky scent and out of the cold wind for a moment.

"Fine. It is all terrible, and you know it. But it doesn't do any good to bemoan our situation. We just have to find another hand of cards to play and keep raising our bet. This isn't a game we can quit, is it?"

He squawked and tipped sideways slightly as Arc gestured for them to fly lower.

"I'll dive in," Arc said over the wind and the sea, "and attempt to get Lilia's attention."

"I still don't like this part of the plan. Just let me jump in. I'm going in anyway. What is the use in stalling the inevitable?"

Because he can light up the water, Daughter. Now, put your heart away for a time and use your mind, Amona said.

She was right, but that didn't mean Vahly had to like it.

Nix's bright eyes flashed in the starlight. *Besides, males love to be a hero. Let the handsome fellow show his worth, and you can reward him later.* She winked.

Arc leapt from Nix's back, a graceful slip into the great stretch of silvery black. Vahly's heart hung limp in her chest as she watched the foam and bubble of his dive disappear.

Stop holding your breath, Amona ordered.

And even though so many other connections and experiences had muffled the Bond she had with Amona, the demand had Vahly exhaling roughly as Kyril circled the area.

Light bloomed beneath the waves, inconsistent but bright—one of Arc's illuminated spheres of air magic. The blurred, golden light moved westward in a straight line, and she was reminded of what great swimmers elves were.

Nix flew beside Kyril. *He'll be fine. If you keep making that face, you're going to age yourself ten years.*

Vahly glared.

He is a fantastic swimmer.

I was just thinking that. It's sometimes pretty annoying that elves are good at everything.

Nix wiggled her eyebrows. *Everything?*

Enough, dragon.

Nix snickered, and her sharp, full-dragon-form teeth showed at the side of her snout, ivory daggers all in a line. *You're going to be fine too, Queenie.*

You think so, hmm? I have my doubts.

Not me. You are the Earth Queen.

I lost the sword, Nix.

Because my silly tail was in the way.

Don't blame yourself.

I do. A bit. But don't look like that at me. I'll live through the ample dose of humility it gives me. I have plenty of arrogance to balance the error.

Vahly laughed. *That you do.* She sighed and ran a hand over the soft feathers on Kyril's neck. He dipped below Nix, then rose, bumping Nix gently, playfully.

Nix gave him a snarl but tapped him with a wing to show she wasn't truly angry. *Lilia will know that spell. This is a solid strategy, Vahl. It is.*

It feels reckless.

Isn't that your middle name?

A chuckle bubbled from Vahly. *Perhaps.*

Well, then. Only you would come up with this plan, because of who you are and what you've suffered. That means it's the way to go. It's fate. I was meant to have a bevy of devoted males trailing my every move. You were meant to save us.

Care to swap fates?

Nix snorted and blew a burst of dragonfire, her eyes twinkling with humor. *No, thank you, dear. No, thank you.*

Arc's light was faint now, and what she thought was him could've only been the moon on the water.

I still see him, Nix said. *He's going deeper.*

Kyril's body rumbled in a comforting purr, and Vahly

pressed her hand against his side, taking his energy and warmth in.

Amona swooped low, startling Kyril a bit. *King Arcturus comes, and he brings two sea folk with him.*

And sure enough, his light approached beneath the wind-cut surface, two trails of foaming water beside him. Then his head appeared above the waves.

"They are in agreement, my queen."

"Good. Ask them if they're willing to travel closer to the shoreline so I can transform back to my human form once the plan either succeeds or crashes miserably."

He disappeared for a moment then broke through the water. "I will show you the place safest for your drop into the sea. Follow my light."

Arc went below, his light moving immediately and the two sea kynd with him. A chill ripped across Vahly's back. She had to try this. There was no choice.

When General Lilia whispered the spell under the water, it sounded nearly the same as when Ryton had—three words that Vahly refused to memorize. This was the only time she would use this magic. Never again. Gills erupted on the sides of her neck. Magic sizzled down her limbs. An invisible weight lay across her shoulders and in her back as she grew as dense as the sea folk, able to walk the sea floor instead of floating. Webbing emerged between her fingers as she flexed them, then blue-green fins sprang from the backs of her hands. Sea magic rushed through her, a sound she now recognized.

She looked into Lilia's scarred face. "It sounds..." Her throat pinched with pain, then the transformation settled. "Your magic sounds like waves crashing on the coast."

Lilia shook her head. "It makes the sound of the currents."

"They sound the same to me."

Lilia cocked an eyebrow, and her mouth twitched. "Ignorant land kynd."

Vahly cracked a smile. "Vicious sea folk."

They gripped one another's forearms, Vahly being careful with the issue of fins, and a strange feeling rose inside her. She moved back a step and studied Lilia's features.

"Thank you for all you're risking," Vahly said. "I won't betray you."

Lilia pulled her into a hug. "I can see why Ryton chose to follow you. I can truly see it now."

Vahly was pretty sure she would've been tearing up if she hadn't been in the ocean. "Can you teach me the spell you use to retrieve your spear? Does it have the word *spear* in it? I wonder if I'll need to tweak the phrasing?"

"The spell uses the word you would call *weapon,* so I believe it might work. Give it a try without your will behind it," Lilia said, bubbles lining her mouth and eyebrows. "Epistrépste mou, óplo."

Repeating the words, Vahly glanced toward the surface where moonlight filtered through the water. Arc was up there with Amona and Nix. His unhappiness at leaving her down here was clear in his bunched lips and the way he'd given her hand an incredibly hard squeeze before swimming away. Suddenly, her gills spasmed, and she choked.

Lilia grabbed her shoulder. "Breathe with gills."

Nodding, Vahly tried to calm down. Blinking, the water cold on her eyes, she tried out the words again with Lilia's instructions on pronunciation.

"Yes, you have it now," Lilia said, looking pleased and glancing at the other sea kynd with her, a blue-haired female who resembled Astraea a bit. "Now use the magic in your words. We will give you space."

They swam off a distance, and she was alone on the shelf of coral, the island's rocky base just a few strokes away.

She imagined the oaken sword far away, dragged by a hand of spelled water. She could see the blade's carvings in her mind's eye, the slope and jut of the oak, the sharp edge and piercing tip. "Epistrépste mou, óplo."

Water rushed in her ears, but the dark water beyond mocked her efforts. She repeated the spell.

Still, nothing.

Lilia swam to her side. "You are not close enough to the weapon. To the sword."

"Proximity is an issue?"

"It is. I would assume Astraea brought the weapon

back to Álikos Castle to show it off before attempting to destroy it. Perhaps if we swim toward the castle at night..."

Vahly nodded. "I can try the spell as we approach. I don't need to get too close, do I? Why didn't you bring this up earlier, the proximity needs of the magic?"

"You are the Earth Queen." She said it with eyebrows lifted like that was explanation enough.

So Lilia believed Vahly could do great things under the water as well as on land. Well, it turned out she had limitations galore.

"I wish your guess had been right," Vahly said. "I'll speak to my team in the air, then we'll move. Immediately."

"Of course," Lilia said before swimming toward the other sea kynd.

Vahly kicked her feet and rose easily to the surface. The water skimmed the top of her head as she began speaking telepathically with Arc and the rest, telling them the next step in their tangled plans.

CHAPTER 29

In her chamber, Astraea blasted the oaken sword with another wave of spelled salt water. The scent of power, metallic and bitter, washed through her gills. She boiled the water, flushing her own cheeks even though she was well past the spell's borders.

But nothing harmed the Earth Queen's sword. The weapon remained whole, unblemished, unbroken despite the hundreds of attacks Astraea had thrown at it.

She had to destroy this sword and break the human's spirit. If she simply flooded the land again, the earth magic might rise and find a new way to disturb her plans. Sadly, many of her army who had the ability to multiply the waters and thus flood the world had died in the fighting. There were too few of them to attempt it now regardless of the oaken sword and the Earth Queen's army.

Snarling in frustration, she went to her closet and removed a vial she'd taken from the Watcher's cabinet before destroying the disgusting pit. The vial was the green of a Jade dragon's scales, glittering and tinged with the look of pure evil. Swimming back to the sword, Astraea worked the cork from the vial. She stretched an arm out over the carved blade. The elf in the artwork there seemed to sneer.

"If you withstand this, weapon, I'll be well and truly impressed."

With careful movements, she poured a drop of the black liquid from the vial onto the wooden blade. The drop sizzled on its path, then landed against the hilt, not a mark in its wake.

"What? But how?" Astraea began to look closer but held herself in check, called up a spell to whisk the drop of deadly potion out of her window and into the currents where it would disintegrate enough to be harmless. Mostly.

Setting the vial in the netted shelves beside her chaise, Astraea chewed on a new idea. "The human will be searching for this. She is working with Lilia. Hmm..."

She circled the sword, thinking and tapping her nails against her spear. What guidance would Lilia give? She'd surely tell the Earth Queen that Astraea had most likely brought the sword here. But what advice would the stupid, self-serving rebel leader give the human about retrieving the weapon?

Astraea stilled. She would suggest using the retrieval spell, the same magic every sea kynd used to bring a weapon back after it had been lost or thrown in battle. Astraea's mind flipped through the possibilities.

Ryton had turned Vahly into one of the sea folk. Lilia would do the same so that Vahly could use the retrieval spell.

She began to laugh, a rolling, ringing laugh that came from the deepest, darkest parts of her soul.

"Oh, you will be reunited with your sword, Queen Vahly. Worry not about that."

At her dressing closet, she found the dress she'd been wearing the day she'd been captured. She removed one long, blonde hair from the pocket and held it to the shimmering light of the nautili positioned around the ceiling of her chamber.

"Perfect."

There was a knock. Astraea pocketed the hair in her loose trousers, then flung open the doors of her chambers to see her guards holding the Watcher's hunched form.

"Yes." She grinned and snatched the Watcher's thin arm to drag her inside. "Did you enjoy betraying your queen, you disgusting wretch? Why the Source gave you the gift of Sight, I'll never know. Such an absolute waste." She threw the crone against the wall and stared into her face. The Watcher's wrinkles deepened around her blind eyes and her withered lips. "Tell me how to destroy it."

"How to destroy what?"

Astraea cracked her knuckles across the crone's face.

Blood snaked into the water. "The oaken sword. You know exactly what. Toy with me again, I dare you."

The Watcher's head turned so that if she'd had her eyes, they would have seen the oaken sword lashed as it was with rope to a stone bench at the far end of the chamber. The nautili cast light over its carved figures. It was just so impossibly ugly. So...earthy. Wood was such a stupid thing for the world to choose as a conduit for such great power. Even obsidian would have been a wiser choice, though Astraea would admit nothing of the sort to anyone. Obsidian was the rock of the Earth Queens. Why wood?

"You have tried your own spells to break it apart?" The Watcher shuffled toward the weapon.

"Of course, fool. They have no effect. Simple violence against the wood does nothing either, though I'm sure if I had ten years with it, the sad material would rot like wood always does when faced with my ocean."

The Watcher knelt beside the sword and ran a pale hand down its blade. She made a strange cooing sound that raised the tiny hairs on the back of Astraea's neck.

"Well, don't sing it a lullaby, old female. Crush the life from it. You know this weapon means the end of all of us. Or didn't your new favorite, Lilia, tell you as much? Did you not see this outcome yourself? I think you're worthless. Yes, I don't even know why I had my guards bring you here. You have lost your power, your wits, your mind. Get out. Get out!"

The Watcher turned slowly. "Your crown is gone, I see."

Astraea grabbed her spear, shouted, and blasted the crone with a vicious current of boiling water. The Watcher remained kneeling, her head cocked like she was studying Astraea and the water around her, as calm as if no magic had been cast at all.

The Sea Queen blinked. The spell hadn't ruined the old female. She shook off the shock and tossed her blue hair. "Fine. Your power remains. You've proven your point. But don't think I couldn't have you torn apart by my warriors. Now, destroy that sword or bid farewell to this life. Or, if you cannot unmake the weapon, bind it to the Earth Queen."

The Watcher's mouth opened. "But it is already bound to her."

"No, I mean bind her to the sword. A true binding."

"A bent sort of magic, that is."

"And you'll do it, or I'll cut out your tongue."

The Watcher smiled.

"What are you smiling for?" Astraea loomed over the Watcher, breathing heavy. The fool always infuriated with her mad mumbling and nonsensical ways. "Just do the binding." She shoved the Earth Queen's hair into the crone's hand. "Bind it tight. I will know if you disobey me. This is your last chance to live what life you have left."

The Watcher pushed the tattered sleeves of her loose robe up her arms and moved her webbed fingers in a slow rhythm, up and down and to the side. With the hair between her finger and thumb, she whispered a spell, too quiet for Astraea to understand.

The Watcher stood. "It is done."

Blackwater of the depths, why was she still smiling? "Good. Now, go. Guards! Get this thing out of my sight before I have to slay it and ruin the water of my own bedroom." The crone began to shuffle away, but Astraea pressed her hand into the Watcher's chest. "Why did you go to the rebels? What did you learn there?"

"I go where the magic takes me, my queen."

"Don't even bother with the title. I know full well you aren't loyal." She gave the crone one last shove before spinning around and swimming to the doors. "Guards! Where are you?"

The guards burst into the room.

"Take this rubbish out of my castle," Astraea said. "I never want to see her face again."

As the guards dragged the Watcher toward the doors, the crone turned and looked at Astraea over one humped shoulder. "Your time grows near, my queen."

Astraea smiled. "That's the first wise thing you've said this day. Indeed, my greatest day is near, Watcher. Soon, the Earth Queen will come for her precious sword. Once she is under my sea, she will die."

And then the Watcher was gone, and Astraea was left with the terrible weapon of her enemy.

"Now," she said, swimming toward the oaken sword, "I think you and I need to take a trip to Scar Chasm. I do think the deepest part of the ocean will do nicely. That, and a boiling spell."

She called up a whirl of water that lifted the sword and carried it behind her as she swam out of the castle, through the courtyard of tall, emerald coral. She had death on her mind and satisfaction in her heart.

CHAPTER 30

Vahly followed Lilia and her cohort Yenn into the deep water on the outskirts of Tidehame. Everything looked different through these sea folk eyes. A bank of black seaweed shimmered like a dragon's hoard below them.

"What is that?"

"Blackgold seaweed," Lilia answered kicking her legs to rotate quickly, glancing at the sparkling growth before continuing onward.

"It's beautiful."

Yenn threw Vahly a nice smile. "Soon we'll pass a stretch of coral that grows in every color of the rainbow, and you should see the veil fish there. The queen collects them to live in her courtyard."

The water was cool and smooth as it flowed over Vahly's limbs and face. Her breathing had regulated to the point where she wasn't worried about suffocating every other minute, and she was beginning to appreciate the sea's treasures. She really did want to help these good sea folk retain their home. She couldn't imagine destroying the dark beauty here.

"We need a way to recognize rebels from the air. During the fight to come," she said. "To avoid friendly fire."

Lilia chewed her lip as she swam next to Vahly. "Perhaps we can dye our spears blue with squid ink?"

"That might work. We'll hold on blue and attack on red. Do you think this ink of yours will last long enough?"

"If we spell it so," Yenn said, eyes on a shark in the distance. Thankfully, it appeared to be headed away from them.

"But that will use more of your power, won't it? You should make sure to visit your kynd's Blackwater well soon," Vahly said.

"We will." Lilia switched her grip on her spear. "I have a set time to visit once my rebels have spread the word."

"What are they communicating?"

"We are trying to persuade more of our folk to join the revolution and to rebel in their own ways."

Vahly's heart lifted. "I hope it works. We'll need all the help we can get."

"Not if we get this oaken sword back," Yenn said. "With that thing, you'll be unstoppable."

"I wish, but no. I can be knocked from my gryphon or hit with a spear just as anyone else."

Yenn shrugged. "I have a lot of faith in you."

"Thanks. Oh, one more thing, General Lilia. I will do my best to attack during the brightest time of day to hinder Astraea's warriors' vision. Is there anything you can do to prepare yourselves for the harsh light and give yourselves an advantage?"

Lilia's forehead wrinkled, and she blinked. "Yenn, any ideas?"

"Maybe we could plaster kollódis leaves across our eyes, leaving small slits so that less light passes into our eyes?"

With a nod, Lilia agreed. "Those leaves will adhere...I think that's the dragon word to use. They will adhere to our flesh. Stick. They will stick."

"Smart. That might actually work," Vahly said, trying to focus on this problem rather than the fear that Astraea was about to swim out of every shelf of rock and coral they swam past.

"Watch out for the breaker fish," Yenn said, grabbing Vahly's arm and urging her deeper as a school of massive silver creatures swam overhead. Another group of fish swam behind them, emerald and thin. "And of course the grassfish are out today. Annoying things."

Vahly started to ask what was annoying about them when a new, slightly colder current rippled across their path.

Lilia held out a hand to stop them. "Try the spell here, Queen Vahly." Her head turned as she watched the water, presumably making certain no one surprised them here.

Vahly envisioned the oaken sword and repeated the spell. Sea magic rushed beside her ears, and its power hummed through her chest, a strange cousin to the feel of earth magic.

Then there was a sharp tug on her ribcage.

She gripped her shirt. "I feel something."

Yenn nodded. "It's working. Say it again. It will come."

Vahly's lips curled around the magic in the spell, and the sensation in her chest increased in intensity, almost to the point of pain. Without thinking, she took off in the direction the spellwork wanted her to go, just as she'd done on land when following her earth magic.

"Wait!" Lilia was soon swimming beside her, eyes wide. "What are you doing? You're swimming in the wrong direction."

"This is the way the spell is leading me."

"No," Yenn said, "that's not how it works. The weapon comes to you."

Lilia took Vahly's arm. Her grip was incredibly strong. "And I'm certain Astraea has the weapon at Álikos Castle. You're headed for the middle of nowhere."

Vahly shook her off, her skin feeling too tight. "I have to do this. This... It's painful." She pressed a hand to her side where the pull was most intense.

Lilia and Yenn exchanged a look, then Lilia spoke.

"Then we'll follow it. Perhaps magic does indeed work differently for the Earth Queen."

Vahly sped off as quickly as she could toward black water lit only by faintly glowing fish the size of a thumb. Lilia whispered a spell over her spear. Magic shushed alongside them, pulling Vahly into a faster pace but reducing the effort required to swim.

Yenn looked past Vahly at Lilia. "We're almost to Scar Chasm."

Lilia twisted. "I don't like this."

Vahly felt nauseated at the incredible power of the pull inside her. "I can't stop. Unless you lash me to something. It's too much." She sucked a breath from the water. If she'd been on land, she'd have been covered in sweat.

They arrived at what Yenn had called Scar Chasm with its glowing shelled creatures and narrow passage. Memories assaulted Vahly. This was where Ryton had brought her to hide her until he had figured out what he wanted to do with her. This was where she had met Astraea face-to-face for the first time.

The absolute darkness yawning from the depths of the chasm spread a layer of ice over Vahly's skin.

"My...my original steel sword is down there. Ryton threw it into the depths."

Yenn rattled off something in their sea language, and Lilia answered, then turned to Vahly. "I'll escort you down there. Yenn will stay here."

Vahly could only nod, the pressure was so painful. She swam quickly toward the deep water, Lilia slipping past to lead in the narrow passageway. Soon, Vahly couldn't see her hand in front of her face. She looked up, or what she hoped was up, and saw the flicker of tiny lights. Or it could've only been in her mind. And still they swam. A chill spread through the water as they traveled deeper, and the water set heavy hands on Vahly's head, back, and limbs. If she'd been in her human form, she'd have been crushed at this depth. Heart tripping over faster beats, she focused on moving her arms and legs, on listening for the rush of magic that guided her.

"Can you still see?" Vahly assumed since Lilia was born to this, she had better vision in the dark water.

"Not much."

Vahly felt Lilia drift to her side.

"Let the magic lead you," Lilia said.

But this spell didn't feel like proper magic, like the power she felt on land or even when she had last been under the sea. This painful tug was rough, unrelenting. She didn't want to say it out loud, but she felt like somehow, someway, she'd been tricked.

"We're approaching the bottom," Lilia said.

Vahly jumped at her voice. Lilia took her arm, and they righted themselves so they were standing, feet on the deadly cold ocean floor. Vahly bent to feel around the bedrock. Her fingers touched on small rocks, drifted through piles of sand, and discovered the hard edge of the chasm's walls, but she couldn't find the source of the pain in her chest.

Swallowing, she tried to look up. Not even those specks of light were visible anymore. Utter darkness had enveloped them in its icy shroud. Magic surged through her, and she lunged forward, foot sliding until she stumbled. She put her hands out to catch herself, a very land kynd type of movement that didn't do much down there, and her fingers touched something hot.

She pulled back, but the magic punched her ribs, and she reached out for the object. "I found something." Lilia's hand was light on her back, a support. Vahly continued delicately feeling out the object. She touched what she thought might be a sword's hilt, but then the water directly around the object grew too hot for her to handle, and she yanked her hand away, hissing. The magic pushed at her, and she nearly put her hand back into the incredibly hot water spinning around the object.

"Tell me what's going on," Lilia asked, her voice tight and low.

"I think this is the oaken sword. But there is an eddy of hot water spinning around it. I can't touch it but the magic...it demands that I grab it." She gritted her teeth so hard she feared her jaw would crack. "The pain...Lilia, any ideas?"

Lilia was snarling in the sea folk language. "My queen. Such a horrible creature. I'm so sorry. I swear to you that we are not all so evil. Astraea has put a binding on the oaken sword. She has bound you to it. She must have taken something of yours to work this magic. Perhaps a hair from your head or a bit of your flesh under her nail."

"It's possible, I guess. We were close on the shore when I was questioning her. How do we break the binding?"

"I don't have any idea. The Watcher would know."

"Where is your Seer?"

"She was with us at the rift, but she went missing. I fear Astraea's guards found her."

"Well, that isn't the answer I was hoping for, Lilia." Vahly coughed or whatever it was down here. It felt much like coughing but also a bit like vomiting. Stones and Blackwater, if she didn't plunge her hand back into that boiling water, she was going to go mad.

Lilia gripped her wrist. "I can scent your desperation in the water. Don't reach your hand in there."

"I can stand the heat for a minute."

"The water will most likely go to a much higher temperature the moment you lock your grip on the sword. I've read legends about such bindings and curses."

"And none of these darling bedtime stories said anything about breaking the magic involved?"

"Our bedtime stories are obviously not as merciful as the land kynd's versions. We raise our younglings to be fierce. So no."

"That's unfortunate, because I'm pretty certain I'm about to die."

"I have an idea."

"I'm listening."

"You grab the sword and shout when you have it. I immediately call up a spell to blast you to the rocky coastline."

"So when I'm boiling to death in a tempest of cursed water, you'll dash my body against the rocks. How is this a plan? Did you switch sides?"

"When you touch the land, you can transform. The curse won't be able to hurt you once you are yourself again."

"You are guessing."

"Very much so."

"I don't suppose we have another plan hiding down here?"

"No."

"Well, all right. Wait. Have you tried the spell where you loose someone like an arrow at the coast?"

"I haven't. But I've seen it done."

"Lovely."

"It isn't a difficult spell."

"What happens if there is a shelf of coral or a shark or Astraea's warriors happen to get in my way as I'm careening through the water?"

"The spell will drag you around them."

Vahly swallowed, her ribs shrieking and her heart seizing. "Let's do it. I can't take this pain any longer anyway. If we wait, I'm going to put my hand into the cursed water regardless. I can't withstand it."

"I'm here. I'm ready. Shout when you have the sword in your hand."

"There are so many things that could go wrong here." Vahly breathed out, and bubbles tickled her lips. "One, two, three…"

She thrust her hand into the hot water and gripped the hilt of the oaken sword.

CHAPTER 31

The cursed water surrounding the sword seared Vahly's fingers as she curled them around the hilt of the oaken sword. Screaming, bubbles rose from her mouth in the black pit of the chasm.

Then Lilia's spell must have taken hold because a wave crashed into Vahly's torso and thrust her upward, taking her breath and stealing the scream from her mouth. She gritted her teeth as the water grew hotter. Her wrist shook as she kept her hold on the sword. Lilia's spelled salt water blasted her up and out of Scar Chasm, and soon she was flying through the sea.

The cursed water hissed like snakes slithering around her grip, and tiny blisters rose on her palm, swollen spots of flesh pressed against the hilt. Her mind buzzed. Pain shattered her thoughts. The only thing that remained constant in her head was the agony and the desire to have Kyril beside her.

"My familiar. My Kyril. I need you," she said into the

water, her words garbled and lost to the sweep of the current.

The sun must have been rising because Vahly glimpsed through squinted eyes the passing views in veils of pale green as light filtered down through the water. But the heat increased and increased, and she thrashed, dying to release her hold on the sword but knowing all was lost if she did. Since the sword was bound to the chasm, and she to the sword, she'd only be pulled back to the chasm along with the weapon to start this nightmare all over again.

The scent of the earth rose in the water, and grimacing, retching, she turned to see she neared the rocky base of the island. The water slid over her. Fast. Too fast. Her entire arm shook, completely out of her control except for her grip. The one true focus. She had to keep hold of the sword no matter what. Her hand felt incredibly swollen, especially her palm and the sides of her fingers. She might lose every inch of flesh on her hand, but by the Source, she was not letting go of the one weapon she could use to end the war and secure every life in the world.

Sure enough, Lilia's spell smashed her into the base of the island, and her spine bent painfully as she rolled against a rock like a fist. Shrieking and masking her pain with rage, she threw her arm forward and thrust the sword's tip into the rock.

"Change me, earth. Change me!"

Power exploded through her, snapping joints and

flooding her with a tingling chill that spread into her burning hand. She exhaled in relief as her fingers and palm left the realm of mind-numbing pain. Hand throbbing, she held on still.

The earth cupped her in molded rock and lifted her through the water as her gills shrank, a tickling along her neck, and her fins faded into nothingness. The water fell away as the earth set her on the grassy shore, high above the seaside cliffs.

A breath of clean air filled her human lungs, and Kyril burst from the sunny sky to snag her shirt and lift her into the air. He flew her all the way to the Sacred Oak, where he gently lay her just beyond its reaching roots and falling leaves.

Another familiar face appeared over her as Kyril nuzzled against her, giving her energy.

"I'm glad you're back," Nix said, smirking and in her human form. "I thought I was going to have to tie your handsome elf to a tree."

CHAPTER 32

A rc stood motionless as Kyril lowered Vahly onto the ground. With Nix at her side, she stood on her own, her golden hair glowing under the rising sun, her cheeks flushed, wiry muscles moving beneath her sleeves, her oaken sword exuding power and gripped in her trembling and reddened hand. Water slicked from her skin and clothing, casting silver droplets onto the tall grasses and Kyril's pelt, and Nix stayed back, no doubt being cautious as Vahly was most likely touched by spelled salt water since she'd been dealing with the Sea Queen's treachery.

She looked every inch a goddess, and he wanted to simply stare at her for eternity.

So as not to look a fool, he forced himself to walk over to her, then knelt. His throat felt tight. He truly had feared the worst. But she was here. Alive. Powerful. "My queen," he whispered, his gaze on her bare feet.

Her cool fingers raised his chin, and she grinned at

him though her eyes were pinched with some worry or some pain. "Rise, my king." She eyed his lips, opened her mouth to say something, but then she closed the distance between them and kissed him fully.

Her lips tasted of the sea; her skin hummed with magic. His body warmed to hers, and he raised air magic to whip a wind around them and dry the ocean from her clothing and hair as they held one another. His body grew rather more insistent, and this was not the time, so he stepped back.

"If you need to tell the story, I will listen. But honestly, I'd rather not. I'd prefer to forget your time away and focus on the attack I see building in your gaze."

She grinned like a wolf and set a hand on Kyril, who walked up beside Nix. "Agreed. But first, can you heal my hand?"

When she released the sword to Nix and flipped her palm up, Arc's stomach dropped. Blisters covered the surface, painful welts that spoke of her trials under the sea.

He immediately summoned healing inside him and sent it coursing into her hand. He pressed a gentle kiss to her wrist. "My love. I'm so sorry. You amaze me again and again."

She tousled his hair with her unmarred hand. "Enough sweet talk. We have work to do." Her girlish grin and the flush on her neck softened her teasing. Arc could tell she was as devoted to and interested in him as he was her.

The four strode quietly to where all the dragons and the three elves had gathered. The Jades remained in their dragon form, while most of the Call Breakers and Lapis had morphed into their smaller forms. Wings shuffled in the autumn wind, and the scent of ripe acorns touched Arc's nose.

Vahly sheathed her sword and walked a path back and forth in front of the quiet crowd while Arc spun air magic to help her voice carry to those standing at the back.

"We will attack in a staggered circular formation."

Amona, in her human form, lifted her chin. "I request the Lapis go in first. The Jades did enough of that for us during the pre-flood years."

Eux's eyebrows lifted, then she nodded at Amona.

"Lapis, you'll become the first curve of the circle, the line that will come at the sea folk head-on. The Jades will complete the circle by coming in from the back in a way similar to what we attempted at the undersea Blackwater well. Mistress Nix, your Call Breakers will dive from above the circle while General Lilia's rebels attack from the bottom of the sea. King Arcturus," her eyes were bright as they gazed at him, and he prayed to the Source he wouldn't disappoint her, "your elves will ride Lapis dragons and combine their air magic with the dragonfire to fight as they see fit. You, my king, will ride with me and Kyril," she said, "so we can increase the capability of the earth gryphons and the sword, combining your air magic with the dragons' magic and mine. Mistress Nix, please accompany us as well."

"You couldn't pry me off your side if you tried," Nix whispered from the front row.

Vahly gave her a look. "Good. Now, my small force will round up the sea folk so we can form the circle around the vast majority of Astraea's forces. Once they are contained and we have them cowering, I will seek out Astraea and give her one last chance to give up her blood for the sword, for the peace."

"What happens when she refuses or if she is killed in the battle?" Eux asked.

"We will do our best, but that is all we can do, Matriarch Eux. If our plans sour, we'll make a new one."

Arc grinned. She was not a usual sort of leader, his Vahly. She didn't put on airs, pretending to be someone she was not. Honesty and courage were her two shining attributes in this new role of hers, and she used them perfectly.

He cleared his throat and stepped forward, hands clasped. "How do we ensure that we don't injure General Lilia and her rebels?"

"Ah. Right. I discussed that with her while I was under. The rebels will hold blue-dyed spears. Only attack those who hold red coral spears."

The dragons whispered among themselves, surely reluctant to withhold fire on any sea folk.

Vahly was talking with Amona and didn't seem to notice the growing trouble.

Arc raised his hands to gain the crowd's attention. "The rebel sea folk are key in our strategy. As you know, they saved us from a sea beast early in our quest to find the sword. And they are the only reason Queen Vahly is here now to fight for us. As Elven King, I swore an oath to them as well." His stomach fluttered with the thought of breaking such a promise. He would never be able to live with himself if he didn't do his best here to protect those sea folk brave enough to fight against their own kynd. "I will uphold my oath. I ask that you find it in your hearts to forgive those rebels their past transgressions and work with them to seek out a new way for us all to live."

He turned to see Vahly watching him with shining eyes. "That is," he said, "as long as my queen agrees."

"I do agree. Wholeheartedly. Anyone I see attacking a blue spear fighter or even being careless with your fire around a rebel, that one will answer to me when this is through."

The crowd bowed their heads, and Vahly swallowed.

Arc came closer, then put a hand on her elbow. The curse's inconsistent pain flashed through him, and he inhaled sharply. She glanced at him, but he schooled his features so she'd never know he was still suffering.

He just had to fight through the battle. Then they could focus on a possible solution. It would be fine. He'd been through worse than this, and she didn't need more to worry about.

"I'm fine," he said, forcing his words to come out smoothly, evenly.

Her gaze touched his forehead, his eyes, his throat. "All right. If you say so." She turned to the crowd. "Ready yourselves for battle. We leave when the daylight will do the most damage to the sea folk's eyesight. We leave when the sun is at its zenith."

Arc trembled as he fought another wave of the crown's curse. He would overcome this. Now was no time to die.

CHAPTER 33

Astraea welcomed her scout Calix into her chamber, then motioned for Larisa to halt her lovely singing. "Please, sit."

Calix frowned, light eyebrows bunching, and glanced at the chaise. "My queen, the tracing spell you set on the oaken sword is awake." He touched his chest.

Grinning, she swam around him. "How does it feel? Does it hurt?" His shoulders were smooth under her fingers, the edge of his sealinen and shell vest shined to military perfection. He'd once worked with Ryton. But now, now he was all hers for this very special mission.

Calix looked down, his jaw working.

Astraea took his lightly bearded face between her finger and thumb. "It's all right. You can tell me."

The whites of his eyes were red, and the veins in his neck grew more pronounced with every moment they stood there. "It is quite painful. But I'd endure this and more for you, my queen."

"Aww. My loyal warrior." She leaned close to his ear. "If you succeed in this, I will reward you beyond imagining." She took his hand and set it on the exposed flesh above her navel. He shivered and swallowed, obviously fully smitten with her, as he should be.

"Larisa," she said taking up her spear, "I'm off. I do hope you'll head into the western waters for a brief respite. This battle will get quite messy, and I want you protected."

Larisa gave her a weak smile. "Of course, my queen."

Sadly, she hadn't been the same since their terrible experience on land. But it was a small cost, those lesser smiles. Nothing could pull Astraea down this day.

The stupid human had taken the bait.

Astraea had known Queen Vahly just loved a challenge and that cursed, boiling water and the binding were the perfect project for her and her foolish rebel cohorts. With all the pain the idiot Earth Queen had surely experienced, she likely had no sense of the tracing spell that had entered her blood through the hand set upon that horrible sword. The very moment she left her beloved land, Calix—the anchor Astraea had chosen for the tracing spell—would feel it like bolt of lightning. And he was plenty strong enough to withstand the jolt.

"Time to turn the seas to blood, Calix. Let us go." She led Calix out of the castle, all the way to the army's training fields past the blackgold seaweed where Echo, a probable spy for Lilia, and General Venu had called up the full army. "Did you find enough new trainees to raise our numbers back to one thousand?" she asked Venu.

"Almost, my queen."

Her nostrils flared. "What number have we gathered here?"

"Eight hundred nine."

The infuriating Earth Queen, her elves, and her dragons had culled nearly three hundred sea warriors in the battle.

Shaking off her disappointment and swimming above the gathered fighters, Astraea held out her spear toward Calix.

"This male is our hero for today. Celebrate him!"

Raising their spears and fists, the army erupted into cheers. Venu gave Calix a respectful nod while Echo just appeared pale around the gills, which made Astraea grin.

"Calix has taken on the role of anchor to a tracing spell I placed on the Earth Queen. When I allowed her to capture me, I stole a hair of hers and set up a binding and a tracing. It was rather torturous for the human to endure, I'm sure." She raised an eyebrow and smirked. The army chuckled, murmuring appropriately about her cleverness. "The spell awoke in him, and now we will follow his lead to where the Earth Queen believes she will surprise us with her piddly dragon force. Come. We leave now."

. . .

ASTRAEA SWAM BEHIND CALIX, Venu at her side and the army trailing in disciplined rows by unit and rank. They had been down the coast past the old human capital of Bihotzetik with its obsidian cathedral, but now the spell on Calix was leading him northward again.

Gritting her teeth, Astraea forced a smile when she turned to Venu. "This relocating will confuse any of Lilia's spies quite well. They will be reporting our location as being anywhere from one end of the island to the other."

"It should prove to confuse the enemy, my queen. Did you read the reports on the pocket of rebels we put down in Tidehame's southern end?"

"I did. All dead now, yes?"

Venu blinked but answered quickly. "Yes."

They swam on quietly, stopping at the Blackwater well to revive their magic before following Calix back to Álikos Castle.

But all was still, normal. Sea folk going here and there as ordered. No dragon or gryphon shadows marred the light coming from the surface.

Pointing at a young female warrior, Astraea said, "You there. Check the surface for approaching dragons."

The female's eyes widened, then narrowed. "Yes, my queen. I am yours to command."

"I like her. What is her name, Venu?"

"Sansya." A darkness flickered over his features.

"What is it?"

"She was one of Ryton's select warriors."

And again the ache of his loss pierced the Sea Queen's chest like a spear. She looked away, toward the castle walls where they'd spent so many nights together in happiness.

"Why did he forsake me, Venu?" she whispered.

"He lost his nerve when Grystark died. Then the Watcher tempted him with false promises. I believe his mind was twisted, broken."

"You're most likely right, General. It is such a sadness to me."

"They are here!" Sansya shrieked.

Then the earth beneath the army buckled.

CHAPTER 34

I n a meadow beyond the Sacred Oak, Vahly drew a line in the ground and asked the earthblood to rise. Birds took flight from the saplings dotting the area, then golden liquid gurgled to the surface. Vahly quickly climbed atop Kyril and left the dragons to it.

As they flew over, Jades, Call Breakers, and Lapis gathered around the five new streams of earthblood, their conversation muted, serious, eyes wary. But the wariness had nothing to do with their ancient feuds, Vahly knew; it was for the upcoming battle with the sea.

She leaned close to Kyril, and his feathers tickled her face. Who among those dragons would be lost today? Aitor stretched out beside Nix, making it so that she could lie back on him, and she did. She must have said something funny because Aitor laughed, bumping Nix's head with his shaking stomach. Nix spread her wings slightly, teasing Aitor and Euskal, who'd arrived with Eux and the rest. Baww dropped down beside them, causing Nix to grin and scoot over for the heavyset dragon. Baww handed them each a container that was surely filled with the strongest dropcider possible. Fifty-one Call Breakers had arrived with Eux, the seriously injured remaining with Helena the healer and Ruda, who Vahly had heard was quickly becoming a true force to be reckoned with.

Beside the Breakers, ninety-seven Jades knotted themselves into groups around the earthblood veins. They weren't much for conversation, keeping to themselves and remaining in dragon form nearly all the time. Eux sat in the center of her dragons, eyes closed and mouth moving in perhaps a battle chant or something of the sort.

The Lapis created a loose line with Amona at the end, and Vahly was glad to see several powerful warriors healthy enough to be here in the ranks. Thirty-eight Lapis had flown from the north to join the fight. That made a total of one hundred eighty-six dragons. Astraea's army numbered in the upper hundreds, nearing one thousand minus the warriors Vahly and her fighters had taken out. The odds were stacked against her and she knew it all too well. It would take a miracle to achieve victory.

She swallowed a bitter taste on the back of her tongue and urged Kyril to land beside the Sacred Oak where Arc waited with Rigel, Haldus, and Ursae. Arc's three subjects had their hands on his arms and back and were, she guessed, giving him healing energy for the battle.

She dismounted. "Can I get a dose of that too? My hand is still a little angry with me for grabbing a cursed weapon."

Quietly thanking the Source for the magic that had raised animals from the healed earth so they could eat, she pulled from her bag a brace of rabbits she'd shot with far too many arrows this morning. She set them out for Kyril's meal. The gryphon went to work on the meat, yellow beak darting here and there. He'd already eaten a deer Arc had gifted him earlier, but Kyril's hunger knew no bounds.

Arc greeted her with a chaste kiss on the cheek, and his large hands briefly circled her waist, his touch sending shivers down her body. He motioned to his subjects, and they began healing her further. Warmth spread through her injured hand, and she flexed her fingers over Arc's wide palm.

"So much better. Thank you."

They set to sharpening blades, filling quivers, and tightening baldrics and belts. Vahly tucked the obsidian knife she'd retrieved into a loop on her baldric, then slid a dagger Rigel had given her into her belt beside the sheathed oaken sword. That done, she paused, hand on the warm leather of her belt and her heart racing.

She had no idea how this would go. Would she know what magic to use when? Would the power inside her lead the way?

Kyril nuzzled her, and she pressed herself against his massive form.

"What if I fail, Kyril?" she whispered into his fur and breathed in his comforting, animal musk.

He sent her an image of the sky, blue and open. It was his definition of hope. She could feel the meaning in the colors and lines of the image.

She smiled into his pelt. "I hope too, friend." With a kiss, she went back to readying for the fight.

Steps away, Ursae blinked and looked behind Vahly. Nix, Aitor, Baww, and Euskal landed gracefully in their full dragon forms. Well, Baww was a touch less than graceful, but he had handled his switch from barkeep to warrior rather well considering his tavern-built body, as Nix always described it.

The various blues of the dragons' wings showed every color of the sky from storm to sunset to noonday. Arc climbed onto Nix's back, silver-haired Rigel slung a leg over Aitor's neck, and Ursae leapt onto Euskal's slim body, using one of his spikes as a handle of sorts. Haldus easily jumped into place on Baww's back, then Kyril bent low to help Vahly up before running to jump into the air.

Kyril's wings spread wide as he soared, leading the entire group of dragons and elves. The land was Vahly's own treasure hoard, the new flowers her rubies, the growing grass and trees her emeralds, and the healthy hills and mountains her gold coins. But unlike a dragon's hoard, this bounty was meant to be shared.

At the foamy coast, not far from the sea folk's

Blackwater well, the units broke apart to work their assigned attack strategies. The Jades and Lapis headed southwest to hover over the distant sea, hopefully out of sight, while Vahly and her group flew toward Tidehame to root out the Sea Queen and her army in the very heart of their watery kingdom.

The ocean spread its wings below them, vast and dark. A silence fell over the group, and a buzzing tension snapped between them.

Arc set his gaze on Vahly, and he nodded. This was it, the place where it would all begin.

Vahly drew the sword of oak and swept it through the air. "Rise, earth, and bring Astraea's castle to me."

Magic surged inside her blood, singing and drumming in her ears. The water exploded in white waves, and the bed of the sea mounded to expose the stone roofs of Álikos, the long windows crowded with broken limbs of glittering green coral, elaborately carved doors swung wide, guards shrieking and swimming to escape the chaos.

Holding up her free hand, Vahly ordered the dragons to hold their fire. They had to do this in a way that had all the sea folk rushing southward, into the trap that the rest of the dragons were currently forming.

The sea spit the tower Vahly had been held prisoner in, its peaked top crumbling as it reached skyward, chunks of flat stone and rounded bricks tumbling back into the hungry waves.

Behind the raucous water around the rising land, a

wave peeled away from the surface, crawling and growing and hissing with magic.

It's Astraea! Nix slid into the air current beside Kyril, and Arc's hands whipped up a sphere of blazing light.

Vahly's hand remembered the burn of the cursed water, and her throat recalled the feel of coinfish. She swallowed hard and kicked Kyril's sides. They rushed through the air toward the growing wave.

The Sea Queen's face appeared like a ghost inside the wave beside three other sea folk, a black-haired male, a female with short hair, and a male whose face was as gray as a corpse's. Below and around them, hundreds of faces showed just under the ocean's border.

Widening her eyes and feigning fear, Vahly pressed a heel into Kyril's right side. He veered harshly and turned them around so they seemed to be fleeing. Vahly flicked her sword at Aitor and Euskal, who blew dragonfire into the remains of the castle and its ruins even as Astraea commanded the ocean to reclaim it. They had to sell this feint if this was going to work. Once the two Call Breakers had flown over, Nix shot fire at Astraea, and Arc threw air magic to back her up. The light made Astraea and her three wince and squint, and the fire had them scrambling to raise more water over the area. The group dipped low, skimming the surface of the unmagicked sea. Nix sped up to trail Vahly.

Still watching over her shoulder, she saw Astraea gaining on them and aiming her spear. The Sea Queen wouldn't miss.

"Low!" she shouted to Kyril.

He dropped so suddenly that Vahly's stomach flew into her throat, and she grasped his ruff, nearly flying from her seat and losing the whole battle right at the start of it.

A spear cut the air above their heads, taking one of Kyril's feathers in its vicious path before dropping to the glistening waves.

Baww and Haldus flew by, a bulky silhouette, and beyond them, Aitor and Rigel, and Euskal and Ursae soared high and fast.

Obsidian hair flying and phantom crown sparkling, Arc whistled as he and Nix flew past. He flashed her a wicked grin. The alchemist-turned-king was enjoying this. He'd gone mad.

She shook her head. "As fast as you can now, Kyril."

Vahly leaned against him, holding on as best she could with legs and her one free hand. She wouldn't sheathe the sword. That darling was staying in her grip until someone pried it from her dead fingers. Wind tore at the three braids she'd woven into her hair that morning, and salt crept into her mouth, sticking between her teeth. Earth magic drummed through her bones and shushed in her veins as they flew hard toward a dark, jagged line in the bright sky.

Amona and the Lapis were ready.

CHAPTER 35

"Up, Kyril. Now!" Vahly held on as Kyril turned his wings in a sharp movement that had them spiraling toward the sun. She looked down to see Astraea and her massive force of sea warriors reacting to the appearance of Amona and her Lapis. The sea kynd broke into five groups, and the fight began in earnest. They conjured a swell large enough to take down all the remaining Lapis. Tentacles of spelled water whipped toward the dragons, and an intense briny odor soured the autumn wind.

Amona's yellow eyes flashed as she breathed a wild river of fire onto the churning swell. Water turned to smoke, and the sea folk on the front lines morphed into charred memories. Amona growled, snarled, and struck again, her Lapis joining in, their fire flanking the wave. Sea warriors threw hundreds and hundreds of spears from the curling blue-black mass, catching two Lapis, who fell screeching into the sea.

The sound of the screams and the roar of Amona's grief-fueled attack curdled Vahly's blood. Fear was a beast on her back that scratched her thoughts and broke them into unusable shards. The other Lapis joined in and blasted the two central units with dragonfire that chased them several feet deep into the water. Spears floated on the black and bloodied water as the units regrouped, the weapons' shafts jutting from the white caps. A spelled wave careened toward Amona, and her neck stretched as she lurched to fly above its killing blow. The tip nearly caught her talons, but she tucked them just in time.

Spears flew after her and the other nearby Lapis. One spear struck a Lapis warrior's underbelly, right at the joint, and the dragon went tumbling to his death, transforming into human form as his scream was swallowed by the ocean and the crackle of more dragonfire to the west.

Vahly wanted to wait to use her power until the Jades came up from the back of Astraea's army so that Astraea wouldn't have a chance to retreat. But the Jades hadn't shown yet.

"Where are they?" She chewed her cheek to bleeding as she traded looks with Arc and Nix, Rigel and Aitor, Baww and Haldus, Ursae and Euskal. "I can't wait any longer. Go!"

Five more Lapis fell into the sea, spears protruding from eyes and soft spots in joints. The air was black with the smoke of dragonfire and the haze rising from burning bodies. Vahly wiped her own stinging eyes as she and Kyril flew in a tight formation with the rest, Arc and Nix not a stone's throw away.

Nose to the sea, Kyril dove closer and closer to the water. Vahly could smell the earth. Even from here, so high, so far away. She could smell its power. Its magic.

"Rise for me!" She waved her sword in a half circle. Somewhere deep inside her, she could sense the crack of earthblood in the seabed; the golden eels of fiery liquid mixed with red-hot molten rock crawled toward them, obeying the oaken sword, listening to her will. Claw-like obsidian walls surrounded the watery battlefield. Kyril roared, and Vahly drew the sword across her forearm. They flew over the northern side of the new black barrier, and she let her blood drip from the sword onto the obsidian. The moment the blood hit the rock, vines burst from the dark creation, emerald leaves shining and spreading, twisting and twining to become one, two— ten full-sized earth gryphons.

Vahly's group flew low over the sea kynd.

"Now!"

Nix, Aitor, and Euskal blew dragonfire at the unit of sea warriors surrounding Astraea in her towering column of spinning, spelled ocean water. Arc threw a shining circle of air magic into the flames, and as the earth gryphons roared alongside Kyril, the new creatures blew green fire.

The green fire sparked against the surface and blackened the sea in a wide swathe of pure destruction.

With no time to even lift their spears, the sea warriors fell under the quick death, still and black as the earth's darkest rock.

Astraea spun herself away from her three close allies. She curled into a spelled wave a stone's throw from the green fire.

Vahly urged Kyril to fly over her. "Concede. Give over your blood for peace, and we can stop now. We can make peace here and end this."

"I'll die before you see me bow at your filthy human feet!"

Astraea raised her spear and launched it at Kyril. Nix soared between the spear and the gryphon, and the Sea Queen's weapon slid past Arc's shoulder, only glancing across his body. Blood soaked his linen tunic and further darkened his leather surcoat, and Vahly jerked her own vest, trying to loosen it, trying to breathe.

Arc waved his uninjured arm. *I'm fine. Fight on.*

"Queen Vahly, watch out!" Rigel's strong elven voice strained against the cacophony.

When Vahly twisted to look, it was too late.

A spelled wave swallowed at least a dozen Lapis and then dragged her and Kyril into its cold arms.

Dashed under the waves, she held tightly to the sword. Kyril was pulled away from her in a current that felt like a thousand punching fists.

She pointed the sword down, or what she hoped was down, and asked the earth beneath the sea to shed its watery cloak.

The water shook. Her head was going to split.

Then the ground was under her back and lifting her with speed into the air. Kyril sputtered and shook his wings beside her. Lapis blackened by spelled water struggled all around. There were so many.

A new roar, like lightning snapping an ancient tree in half, echoed across the obsidian-caged battlefield.

Eux and her Jades had arrived.

Nix flew past. Blood streamed from a cut along her back leg.

"Up, Kyril! Now!" Arc shouted. "To the skies!" Arc sent a rousing blast of air magic at Kyril, drying his wings so that when Vahly jumped onto his back, he was able to lift off.

The Jades breathed fire into Astraea's ranks, but still the Sea Queen gave no indication of relenting. Vahly drew the sword in a cutting motion across her view of the far side of the obsidian walls, then slashed it backward, willing the earth to rise again, higher now.

The ground shivered and mounded within its black walls, and soon the thousands of sea warriors, Astraea included, were beached on a new island, laid bare to the fire of the sun.

They gasped and seized, most spears dropped and forgotten in their desperation to breathe. Some clawed at their gills. Mouths worked to no avail.

"Please, Astraea," Vahly called out over the horror. "Submit to the balance and save them. Save your kynd and your foolish self!"

The Sea Queen lifted her spear, and a wave crashed over the island. A tide sucked the sea folk over the edges of the obsidian, and just like that, they had escaped.

Vahly shouted and kicked Kyril's sides, feeling his anger in tune with hers as they flew hard to meet the recovering army with their earth gryphons, green fire, and the dragons quickly regrouping to attack with talon and flame.

Whipping the sword over her head, Vahly imagined the stone gryphon, and he rose from the ocean like he'd been sleeping there since the beginning of time. The stone gryphon joined the rest of the army, and his breath was mere smoke until Arc spun two massive spheres of inky haze and blinding white and threw them. The stone gryphon's smoke shimmered into a blaze of amethyst and sage that ripped the waves from the surface like flesh from a kill and obliterated any living thing in its path.

Astraea whirled her spear as she spun just beneath the sunlight surface. A mighty wave rose beneath the stone gryphon. Arms of spelled water reached for the creature, but he reared back. His wing cracked Amona across the back. She tumbled through the sky.

Once she hit that water, she would be dead. Thick magic swirled in those depths, and not even the most powerful of the dragons could survive submersion there.

Head going light and vision spotty, Vahly pointed to the water under her mother. The largest of the earth gryphons shot between his stone counterpart and the spelled wave and grasped Amona's leg in its talons. Amona managed to get her wings moving, and the earth gryphon released her. They flew high as the spelled wave crashed under the stone gryphon.

Vahly nearly collapsed on Kyril's neck. Then blue spears jutted from the water. She held her sword upright. "Hold fire!"

The rebels had arrived and were engaging Astraea's fighters, spelled water flying like arrows back and forth, spears driving over and above, striking chests, ripping bodies.

A flash of movement caught her eye. Lilia jumped from the water, blue spear outstretched, a slitted and dark leaf across her eyes. She launched her spear toward Astraea.

CHAPTER 36

Veiled in spelled water, Lilia threw her ink-dyed spear at Astraea and spat the spell again. Every beat of her heart said her lost love's name. Grystark. Grystark. Grystark.

"You will pay, beast."

The spell wrapped around the spear helped it dodge Astraea's defensive slash, the move Lilia had seen the Sea Queen do time and time again while she waited on Grystark to be done with the day's training. Blade spinning, the spear flew through the air and lodged in Astraea's leg. The hag laughed as blood poured out of the wound and she tumbled backward into the deep water. Another wave lifted the Sea Queen as she was ripping the spear free. She locked her gaze on Lilia, and for the first time since the night Grystark had died, Lilia felt the cold grip of fear crush the heat of her rage.

But then Astraea disappeared into the water.

Lilia whipped her spear and conjured a wave to send her crashing after the evil queen.

In the rush of falling water, Lilia blinked to see clearly. "Where is she?"

She turned left, right, but only saw glimpses of the fight—a male warrior swimming high to throw a spear at a low-sweeping Lapis, Yenn shooting a blue-tipped spear through the water to strike Astraea's General Venu.

Treading water, Lilia whispered a spell over her spear and threw her weapon to follow Yenn's. Venu dove backward and avoided both weapons. Lilia and Yenn called their spears back, but Venu was fast. He dragged his spear through the currents and the blood-stained eddies, and a spell thrust Lilia and Yenn out of the battlefield and pinned them against a wide hand of sickly green coral as their weapons finally found their hands.

Venu noted their position, then turned to dodge a blast of dragonfire. Vahly must've released the hold. They had to move fast, or they'd be burned alive alongside their enemies.

As they'd practiced, Lilia and Yenn took hold of one another's spears, each gripping their own and the other's, forming a powerful rebounding effect for the spellwork on the weapons. They chanted their magic, and Lilia's spear shook with the intensity of the spell. No single spell would deflect these strikes now.

Spinning, they threw their spears as one and struck Venu in the back.

He was dead before he knew what hit him.

Astraea plunged into the water, and Lilia nearly dropped her returned spear.

"Been playing with the dragons up there, my queen?" Lilia layered her words with venom.

Astraea was bleeding freely from the wound in her leg, but she spun her spear faster than any sea kynd. "I like to let them pretend they're winning." Gashes along her chest and left arm showed the mark of talons.

Astraea threw her spear. Yenn shrieked as the tip plunged into her chest. Lilia's only friend went still, eyes wide and unseeing.

Her vision shrank to a point, and she only saw Astraea's lips as they moved in a spell that would send Lilia to meet Yenn in the afterlife.

Summoning memories of Grystark and Ryton fighting together on the training field, laughing with her in the kitchen, of Grystark's deep, kind voice in her ear, Lilia forced herself out of the panic, gripped her spear, and launched herself out of the water and prayed her voice would be strong enough to shout over the battle's din.

She locked eyes with Vahly. "Strike here, Earth Queen!"

CHAPTER 37

Vahly shouted at Baww, who'd fired in the rebel's fighting zone, then she wheeled Kyril around to direct the stone gryphon at the fourth unit of sea warriors going hard against Eux, her Jades, and a handful of Call Breakers.

Nix flew past. On her back, Arc narrowed his eyes, and his fingers worked a spell. The next time Vahly glanced his way, he wielded a net of sparkling magic, casting it across the sea kynd and lifting them from the water where they gasped and snarled, weakly throwing spears until Eux lit them with a focused beam of intensely red fire.

Euskal breathed flames at a hulking sea kynd male who wielded a two-headed spear. The sea kynd slipped back into the sea, avoiding the blaze, but rose again immediately and took aim. On Euskal's back, Ursae spun air magic and launched it at the male. The light made him call out and cover his eyes. Euskal roared and released a rippling stream of bright orange flame, and the sea kynd went up in smoke.

Haldus and Baww fought with air magic and fire, blasting divots in the waves and sending sea kynd swimming. A sea kynd with a blackened arm rose behind them.

"Baww! Behind you!" Vahly called.

The sea warrior pushed his spear forward, and a wave crashed over Baww and Haldus, dragging them under. Kyril flew low, and Vahly frantically searched the water, only to see them driving out of the water ten feet away, struggling but alive.

A voice cut through the noise, and Vahly turned to see Lilia blasting from the sea.

"Strike here, Earth Queen!"

Though Vahly couldn't see Astraea, she trusted Lilia. She flipped the oaken sword and drove the tip down beside Kyril's heaving sides. "Bring forth your fire, earth. The Sea Queen will not bend, and so she will burn."

The ocean vibrated, and the magic pressed against Vahly's heart and filled her nose with the scents of new, green shoots, summer-singed ground, the musk of animals and dried grasses.

"You will never end me," Astraea's hissing voice sounded as she broke the surface, cheeks pale as quartz and eyes flat black.

A bolt of earthblood shot through the water and into the sky. The flow of molten earth wrapped Astraea like a golden cloak. The Sea Queen's mouth opened in a scream.

Then she was no more.

Vahly's heart thundered, and she gripped her sword, shaking.

Kyril roared, and the dragons joined him, but her stomach turned. She'd killed their chance at balance, and no one knew the true consequences.

The waves ceased.

In the unnatural silence, the water became like glass, blood swirling under the smooth surface around the sea folk who had stilled. Thunder rolled, growing stronger as the sky darkened.

"The sun..." Arc was saying as Nix soared over Kyril slowly. Arc's skin had gone ghostly white.

A bloody hue spread across the sun, and pewter clouds swarmed the skies.

Frost iced Vahly's spine. Whatever this was, it wasn't good.

Two sea kynd males shouted out, pointing. A teeming mass of sea creatures swam closer. Large, triangular fish with whipping tails, sharks with silver-tipped fins by the hundreds, bright teal eels slithering all moved in circles around the vast majority of the sea folk, Lilia and her rebels included, their blue spears bobbing in the dead water. A whirlpool formed, spinning suddenly faster and faster.

What do we do? Nix asked.

"I...I don't know."

The whirlpool centered around one soul.

Lilia.

The rebel leader looked up at Vahly, eyes bloodshot and wide. "Earth Quee—"

The sea sucked her down.

In the sky, the clouds drew to a halt, the sea creatures hovered in the water, and the whirlpool froze like time itself had stopped.

All remained quiet. In the air. In the sea.

There was movement on the distant coast. "Arc, can you see what that is?"

Nix didn't fly him far, and Vahly was glad of it. When they returned a moment later, Arc swallowed and wiped his forehead with a hand. He was sweating. "Animals. Horses. Birds. Mice. Deer. Bears. They've come to watch."

A boom sounded through the ocean like the thunder from above had crossed into the water. The whirlpool and the creatures reversed themselves. A great crack split the air.

Lilia was thrown out of the whirlpool's center.

The sea folk gasped as Lilia's head fell back, mouth open as a spool of dark water thrust her upward. Her finned arms and legs were limp, and her eyes were closed.

The sun peeled back its ruddy cover and blazed over her as the water cradled her and brought her lower, closer to the ocean's surface.

A male sea kynd with a wild red beard rose on a crest

of water and shouted in the sea language. Others answered him in sharp tones, gesturing at Vahly, but she had no idea what they were saying.

Lilia lifted her head and opened her eyes. Between her eyebrows was a mark Vahly recognized immediately.

She was Touched, the place on her brow a shimmering black just like the one that marked Vahly, Amona, and Eux and like the one that had shown on Astraea's flesh as well.

Hope lit a spark inside Vahly. "Kyril, go to her," she whispered. They flew over the wave that supported Lilia like a waterfall-turned-throne.

The sea creatures who had drifted away returned and swam around Lilia, weaving in and out of the fallen warriors and dragons, not disturbing the dead but simply coursing slowly, their movements seemingly focused on the living.

The sea folk raised their voices in a chant. "Genniétai mia néa vasílissa. I thálassa échei milísei." They repeated the chant over and over, their voices bubbling through the water that covered their faces or vibrating in the water, sending ripples across the still surface.

Arc's voice rang in Vahly's head. "They say, 'A new queen is born. The sea has spoken.'"

Kyril's feathers fluttered in the wind, and thunder rumbled before a fork of lightning lit Lilia's serene face. She was their new queen.

She can stop this, Vahly said to Arc. *With her blood, she can balance the world.*

Vahly bumped Kyril's sides with her heel, and they soared over Lilia, the sea creatures, and the chanting sea folk.

"I, Vahly of the Land, respect the sea's choice. All hail our new Sea Queen!" Shouts sounded from the air and the water. "Queen Lilia, will you give a portion of your Touched blood to the oaken sword to restore the balance?"

Lilia blinked, seeming to come back to herself as she watched Vahly fly. "I am reborn," she said quietly before speaking to her people, her words in quick sea tongue. Then she looked up again. "Queen Vahly, I offer my blood." She reached an arm beyond her veil of water, then drew a nail down the inside of her elbow.

Vahly urged Kyril to swoop low. She extended the oaken sword as they passed, and Lilia dropped three perfect drops of ruby blood onto the carved blade.

Emerald light flashed across the ocean and into the sky, there and gone in a blink.

Wind rushed across the sea and cooled Vahly's cheeks. The waves resumed their movement, and the sea surged up slightly before returning to its former level, as if the ocean had taken a great breath of relief. The sea creatures hurried out of the crowded battlefield-turned-ritual sanctuary. Rays of sunlight spread over Lilia, sparkling across her Touched mark as she withdrew, slipping under the surface.

Vahly and Kyril flew up and around to face the

crowd. Vahly herself felt reborn, as if anything were possible.

"Rejoice in the peace we will create!" she called out over the crowd of sea folk, dragons, and elves.

Calls of joy rose from the sea folk, celebratory waves rising and splashing. The dragons wheeled in the sky, roaring their approval in the sunlight.

Vahly waved the sword of oak, and her dragons and their elven riders flew alongside Kyril back to the land, to home, to the new world they had crafted with blood, heart, and magic.

CHAPTER 38

At the Sacred Oak, they dismounted and embraced. But in the crowd, Vahly couldn't spot Arc anywhere. She accepted congratulations and well-wishes with quick arm shakes and words as she wove through the groups.

Nix? Where are you both?

At the far side of the oak. Come quickly.

The urgency in Nix's voice had Vahly running. She tried to push past a group of Jades who grabbed her by the shoulders to praise her courage in battle.

"Thank you. But I must go. Sorry."

They grumbled as she forced her way through their bulky, green bodies. Amona walked up as she cleared the Jades, the last of the Lapis at her side.

"Daughter, your ingenuity in the fight was nothing short of genius." She pulled Vahly into a rare hug, and Vahly gritted her teeth, wishing she could enjoy the moment but worried for Arc.

"Thank you, Mother. But Arc..." She glanced at the tree, trying to see over the crowd. "Nix says to come quickly."

Amona put a hand to Vahly's back and ushered her through the dragons. "Make way for your queen." Amona's voice held the ringing tone of a command, and the clustered Jades cleared a path to the oak.

Rigel's silver hair peeked from the other side, and Vahly rushed forward. Rigel, Aitor, Ursae, Euskal, Haldus, and Baww gathered in a circle. She wiggled through to see Nix on the ground in her human form wearing a loose cloak and cradling Arc's head in her lap.

Nix looked up at Vahly, tears shining in her bright eyes. "I'm afraid we'll have to give him up to the earth soon, darling. Please, come take my place."

Vahly's chest caved. Arc's face was ashen, his eyes shuttered. Blood crusted his hair and stained the left side of his face, and where his surcoat had ripped along his shoulder, bruises marred the luminescent skin. But he wasn't inert due to some battle injury. He was suffering from the curse.

She slid into Nix's place and gently supported Arc as best she could considering her sea-wet trousers and bloodied boots. She pushed a lock of his thick, black hair behind one pointed ear. The ghostly light of his crown didn't seem diminished when she studied it from the corner of her eye. His chest moved with a shuddering breath. She lifted his hand and gasped. Black lines crisscrossed his fingers and forearm, almost all muscle and tendon withered to nothing. The lines inched up his arm toward his neck. She didn't need anyone to tell her what would happen if the curse made it that far.

"What can we do?" she whispered to him, a chill running over her skin. "Don't hold back. Suggest your wildest idea. You know I love a longshot bet, love."

He opened his eyes a fraction, the sparkling, dark color an arrow in her chest. "The only hypothesis..." His eyes closed, and his words fell into silence.

She gave him a gentle shake. "No dying, elf. I've told you. I'm your queen. This is an order." She wiped tears from her cheeks. "Tell me your hypothesis."

His throat moved, and his eyes shifted under his closed, plum-shaded lids. "Destroy the crown."

Vahly looked up and locked eyes with Rigel, then Haldus. "How do we destroy the crown?"

Rigel's lips parted, but instead of speaking, he only shook his head.

Haldus glanced at the elder elf. "As far as we know, the crown cannot be destroyed."

Rigel exhaled and gazed into the wide boughs of the sacred oak. "I don't know how." Then he stared at her. "Perhaps your sword could do the job?"

Nix crossed her arms, tears still hanging on her cheeks. "But how is she going to smash a crown currently on the brow of her beloved?"

"Give me the crown." Ursae stood. She'd been kneeling beside Arc, silent and weeping. "Then kill me. I deserve it."

Vahly grabbed her arm. "No, you don't. You fought well today. You have been on our side. You're forgiven. No one is making themselves a sacrifice. I don't want that, and I know sure as the Blackwater that King Arcturus doesn't want that."

She felt the slightest tightening in Arc's fingers where they circled her wrist as if he were agreeing with her statement.

"Surely elves have been dethroned for noble reasons in history. They've shucked the crown for a cause other than treachery or death. Surely. Rack your brains, elves! Dragons! Give me ideas."

She sounded broken. She didn't care. To finally have defeated Astraea, to have a life laid out in front of her, then to lose him...

"Rigel, please support him." She gave up her spot to the elven elder, then stood and removed her sword.

"Please let this work," she whispered against the carved blade.

With careful movements, she lowered the oaken sword onto what she hoped were the outer edges of the air magic crown. Rigel gave her an encouraging nod.

Panic crawled up her chest, but she pushed it down and closed her eyes to focus on her magic. Words sprang to her lips, and her Blackwater mark tingled.

"Rise, earth, and reclaim the crown of air. Let its power sleep in your dark recesses until the time is right."

Vahly opened her eyes. Nothing had changed. The

crown remained on Arc's head, and his chest had stopped moving.

Rigel rubbed Arc's chest. "My king. Wake, please. Your queen is here."

But Arc's hand slid from Rigel's grip.

Heart dropping, Vahly forced herself to breathe deeply and shut her eyes. "Rise, earth," she repeated, feeling the magic curl around the syllables of every word, pressing her will into every sound. "Claim the crown of air. Break its hold on the soul I choose."

Nix was kneeling and weeping now, her hands on Arc's leg. Aitor's hands braced her shoulders.

Amona stood above Arc, her eyes turned down at the edges. "Vahly, perhaps you should sheathe your sword and say farewell."

The black lines of the curse tangled around Arc's jawline and over his cheeks.

Amona's words cut Vahly like the sharpest blade, but Vahly shut her eyes and tried again. She would never stop trying.

"Rise, earth and all your spirits! Claim the crown of air! Break its hold on the soul who saved me, who heals me, who will forge a new embodiment of elven power! This is my fate, and I choose it! Rise, earth, and claim the crown!"

Power sizzled up her arms from the hilt, then flashed in tingling sparks down her legs. The ground quaked and broke open, spilling fresh water. Opalescent light swirled out of the turned earth and new spring.

Amona, Nix, Aitor, and the rest moved aside, coming to stand next to Vahly. The dragons beyond the oak grew quiet, only whispering and pointing.

The scent of earth magic was pungent and powerful. Salt and minerals. The forest floor after a rain. Sun-warmed fields.

The opalescent light coalesced into human-like forms, and suddenly Vahly was staring at a crowd of galtzagorri, short and ghostly, who had materialized alongside a circle of moonlight. Scales glittered at the edges of the circle. It was the Spirit of the River. To the Spirit's left, a tall, dark, and spindly shadow appeared, perhaps a sort of magical echo of the Mountain Spirit who had given Vahly a sprig of pine what felt like one thousand years ago.

"Greetings, Queen Vahly and King Arcturus." The Spirit of the River's voice was wind chimes and water bubbling over smooth stone.

Vahly bowed her head at the Spirit but kept a good eye on Arc.

"We come to your aid," the Spirit said, reaching a tendril of moon-white glow toward the crown. "King Arcturus will remain king, but he must use his power to forge a new diadem before his end."

"I will help him in his efforts. He will do it. I swear it." Vahly knelt, lifted her sword, kissed the hilt, then held it across her palms toward the Spirit.

A coolness washed over her scalp, then she glanced to see the Spirit's circle growing larger and wavering.

Smudges of darkness appeared at the being's borders like an artist had shadowed the appearance with charcoal. Then the light went purely white again, and Arc's eyes flickered open.

The galtzagorri set their hands on the ground, and a vibrant green light shot through the grasses and dirt. The light flowed into Arc, who jolted and inhaled. The black lines of the curse slithered back down to his fingertips, then disappeared altogether. Vahly flung herself on him and held his face in her blood-stained hands. His color returned, warm and healthy, and the bruises on his shoulder faded.

Tears flowing freely, Vahly faced the spirits. "Thank you."

The ghostly forms bowed as one. Their forms spun into that pearly fog again, and then they were gone.

Arc sat up, and Nix hugged Aitor tightly as Amona whispered a prayer to the Source.

Vahly couldn't breathe. "You are so lucky your hypothesis proved true."

Arc's eyebrow slanted. "Why, were you going to kill me if I died?"

"Exactly that."

"And how would that be accomplished?" He chuckled, his gaze on her warming her middle and making her heart forget how to beat.

"You'll have to glean the secret of double death from me with favors."

"Oh." He brushed her hair from her neck, sending

shivers across her skin. "What sort of favors do you demand?"

She leaned toward his pointed ear. "The talk is that elves are good at everything."

One by one, Amona, Nix, and the rest bowed and left them on their own.

"Everything? That is high praise." He tapped his lower lip with his fist and narrowed his eyes. "I'm sure I read a scroll about this rumor."

"Sack the scrolls, elf, and kiss me."

Arc pulled her flush against him and pressed his mouth to hers, and she quickly forgot about spirits and swords, battles and victories.

It was past time to start a new life woven with the magic of elves and the fate of dragons.

H igh on a wooden ladder in the center of a massive cave, Vahly dragged the obsidian blade in a circle, carving out another name along the wall. Her goal was to cover the feasting hall she and Arc had chosen with the names of those who had lost their lives in the war, and to do the work without magic. She normally had others helping her, but most of the dragons were hunting for tonight's celebration of Frostlight.

Nix walked in, then jiggled the ladder. "Arc is doing something wrong."

Nearly slipping, Vahly glared, then climbed down and flexed her sore hand. "What do you mean?"

"You've only been mated for one moon. You shouldn't have nearly this much energy." Nix hooked her arm in Vahly's. "I'll have to talk with him."

"Nix."

"Or perhaps it's you who is lazing about in the bedchamber?"

"Please, stop." It wasn't often someone could make Vahly blush. She poked Nix in the side and hurried past her. "And if you really want my holiday to go well, you'll cease your prying so I'll have time for a bath."

Now that she had a newly constructed tavern to call her own, Nix was her old self. Incorrigible. Loud. Vahly grinned, remembering how Nix had caught Euskal cheating at dice and made him go to one knee to beg forgiveness in the form of outright flattery and beautiful lies. Yes, Nix was Nix again. Practically perfect.

Chuckling, Nix smacked Vahly's backside as she began to walk away. That dragon was impossible. A tug on Vahly's heart suddenly stopped her and turned her around to face Nix. She hugged her fiercely.

Patting Vahly's back, Nix exhaled slowly and relaxed into the embrace. "What is this for?"

"I never could have done any of this without you. Do you know how much Sugarrabota owes you? How much I owe you?" She drew back and saw tears shining in Nix's eyes.

"You don't owe me a thing, my dear friend. You and your elf have given me back my life. As for the island as a whole, any who care to show their thanks may demonstrate their gratitude with mounds of scorchpeppers and skins of northern wine."

"I'll be sure to announce that at the feast tonight."

Nix bowed. "My queen."

"My Mistress of Festivities." Vahly gave her a grin and walked on.

The cave that served as the feasting hall led into a corridor of stacked stone where torches lit the walls and lapis tiles lined the floor. Breaking into three branches, the corridor led outside, to the kitchens, or to the spirit oak palace, depending on which way one chose to go. Vahly walked into the spirit oak, so named for the pale undersides of its leaves and for the ones who had given Arc his life. She had drawn the oak from an acorn to its full size in the week after the victory over Astraea. The tree towered over the coastline, a mountain almost itself. The sea breeze coming through the arched, carved windows in the new oaken palace smelled fresh and promising, no longer a scent to fear.

Below the outcropping on Lapis territory where she and Arc had made their home, she could see Queen Lilia's gift. The Lost Valley was lost no more. The land was bare in the place where Vahly had been born and the last of the humans had died, but shoots of green were popping up every day, and soon it would be a place for dragons or the elves to settle if they chose. Vahly had a secret wish: that someday the children she and Arc might have would build a city there and she would live to see a new version of her kynd and his rise.

In her bedchamber on the top level of the oaken palace, Vahly crawled into a deep bath perfumed with teal-green rose petals and lavender. Arc had designed a pulley system to lift fresh water from the underground spring. It poured from a stone basin after rising through hollow marsh reeds. Helena had given up healing since Ruda seemed more than capable of taking over despite her young age. The old healer had requested the position of serving Vahly. Vahly still felt guilty when Helena heated the stone tub with her well-controlled dragonfire and brought her flatbread and cider from the kitchens, but Helena insisted the work pleased her, that she was honored to serve a queen. Nevertheless, Vahly did her best not to ask for help more than once a day.

Steam rose from Vahly's bath, and she sank lower, letting the hot water wash the grit from her skin and scent her hair with the thick layer of rose petals and lavender buds that floated on the surface. The quiet was nice. Preparations for Frostlight had been near frenetic with the Jades nearby, camping in luxurious tents in the Red Meadow and always wanting to spar, and the younglings running all over the place and begging for sweets.

"What's this?" Arc's voice made Vahly jump. He sat on the side and trailed a finger through the flowers drifting along the surface. His crown was back. Well, it wasn't the first crown, of course, but the new one he'd fashioned with help from his fellow elves. They'd kept their ritual rather secretive, even from her—something about gathering under the full moon and speaking to the wind. The crown flickered just out of sight, darker than its predecessor with more swirling wisps of deep plum and smoky gray dancing between the threads of sun-bright gold.

She propped a leg up beside him. "This, my love, is the solution to all of your problems."

He laughed fully then, his head back and the apple in his throat moving. Source in the well, he was beautiful. "How is a bath capable of readying the entirety of Sugurrabota's populace for Frostlight?"

Vahly grabbed his loose linen shirt and pulled him closer as she clicked her tongue. "Those are not your problems."

"And I suppose you are going to tell me about mine."

"It's my job as your mate to watch out for you. Stress is your problem, King Arcturus. Now get your fine rear in this tub and we'll see what happens."

He stood and pulled off his shirt, showing his flat stomach and rolling muscles.

"You are doing that on purpose," she said, her throat going dry.

"Doing what?" He narrowed his eyes and disappeared behind the wooden divider by the handwashing basin.

Vahly chuckled and submerged herself. Then the water sloshed and Arc was in the bath, black hair slicked back and water droplets on his sharp chin and pointed ears.

"Well, I am here." His voice was teasing and low. "Are you certain you're prepared for my solution to all of your problems?"

She leaned forward and brushed her lips over his as he curled his hands around her neck gently. "Of course I am. I am a queen."

And just like that, Vahly was at last perfectly happy with not being a dragon.

I hope you enjoyed the Dragons Rising series as much as I loved writing it! If you'd like a bonus scene from the books, series wallpaper for your computer or phone, three free reads from me, and exclusive signed book giveaways, join my newsletter at
https://www.alishaklapheke.com/free-prequel-1

Thank you for reading Sword of Oak. The Dragons Rising series has been incredibly exciting for me as a writer and I am almost positive my next series (a fantasy romance between a water mage and an elven mage) will take place around 3,000 years after this book. It will be title Enchanting the Elven Mage and should release in the winter of 2020.

See you soon,

Alisha

Curious about my other books?: Here is an excerpt from my Forest of Silver and Secrets (Uncommon World Book Four).

Get ready for sea magic...
~Kinneret~

THE PEWTER CLOUDS swung low and balled like fists as Kinneret turned the stubborn wheel, the wood smooth under her calloused hands. She wished to let the ship go where it may, let the storm have them for a bit to keep damage down, but there was no time for that. They had to be at the main Silvanian port before the most powerful merchants went off for their seasonal hunts along the northern coasts and the Northern Isle folk sailed back into their foreboding region. The Silvanian king would leave for his country estate very soon.

Wind whipped Kinneret's hair around her face. Salty water dripped into her mouth. "Sails down. Tie them up. The wind will take them and we'll be headed under."

Calev and five fighting sailors battled the jib sail's tie. Its end cracked across the deck like a great whip, then circled back. Against the ship's side, it snapped and tripped two sailors who landed hard on the planks. That jib sail needed to come down. Now.

The reedy man in the sky cup climbed down the main mast and hurried to help another sailor knot the lines securing the foresail. Thunder echoed across the unending horizon. A school of fish rippled beneath the waters' surface.

From the stern, Oron gave Kinneret a nod. It was time for Salt Magic. Though the magic never worked as well outside the Pass's cursed waters, it was worth a try.

"Take the wheel, Ridhima."

The woman slid into place, long-fingered hands curling over the indents where Kinneret's had just been.

"Watch it, kaptan!" Calev shouted.

The jib sail's line zipped over Kinneret's head. She ducked. Calev leapt and snagged the tie right out of the air.

Water chilled Kinneret's feet through the spaces in her sandals. The soft, leather bag of salt on her sash was full and ready. She drew out a handful and threw it above her head. The storm snarled like an angry desert lion and swallowed her offering whole.

"Wind and rain,
Strength and pain,
Sea, I hear you,
Sea, I see you.
Sail and dodge,
Push and pull,
Sea, hear me,
Sea, hear me."

The wind sounded different here, storm or no storm. They'd left the Pass now and this stretch of water felt like a stranger, one with a familiar face, but a foreign voice.

A wave reached high and crashed against the jib sail. The ship moaned.

Oron shouted through the open door that led below deck. "All hands! On deck now!"

Sailors streamed onto the deck, some half-dressed with just one boot or missing a shirt.

Oron grabbed the two closest. "Forget tying. Just cut the jib loose. Now!"

They rushed across the deck toward the sail at the bow, pulling knives from their sashes. Everyone else clutched onto posts or the masts. Two sailors lashed down the sealed barrels of Old Farm's finest wheat heads —they'd kept that part of the load above deck to watch for mice. Calev and Oron tied themselves and several others to the main mast.

Raindrops thickened into a deluge. Water drummed onto the decking and soaked Kinneret through. The Salt Magic had to work. She was not about to die from a storm at sea after all she'd been through. No. Even if they were out of the main waters of the Pass and far from where her magic thrived.

Lightning flared from above. A crack sounded, and all heads turned toward the sky cup. A jagged line marred the foresail mast, but the support held. If that mast broke, it would come down on the sailors like a giant hammer and most likely punch a mean hole in the ship. Kinneret gripped a post and clung on, her heart hammering. Shouts and prayers rose from most mouths, from Calev, Oron, and the others tied to the neighboring mast. The sea growled and raised a gray-brown hand to strike again.

Clutching the ship like a friend she'd learned to trust with her life, and keeping her gaze on Calev, Kinneret breathed the wet air in. She closed her eyes, reached into her bag for more salt, and shouted another prayer.

"Sea, be with me,

Hear me, see me..."

The wind ripped the grains from her palm and hissed. It felt like a reluctant agreement.

The ship tilted, then evened out as the rain turned into a drizzle on Kinneret's upturned face. Her shoes grated against the decking and someone called for help.

Opening her eyes, she dared to hope. The clouds broke apart to show the sun. The sea smoothed into rolling hills below. The Salt Magic had worked. But barely.

Check out all my books at http://www. alishaklapheke.com

CPSIA information can be obtained
at www.ICGtesting.com
Printed in the USA
LVHW090440010221
677989LV00008B/636